The Shadow's Sister

TALES OF THE FAE BOOK I

KATE SEGER

Tales of the Fae

Book I

The Shadow's Sister

Kate Seger

Contents

Prologue

Blood Born

Shadow Empress Alize writhed on the cold marble, parted thighs slick with viscera, onyx skin gone ashen with the strain. Her screams were sharp as knives, full of dark magic as they severed the silent night. Her cries ensorcelled Castle Bleak in a web of shadows that blotted out the twin moons and the stars above until there was only darkness.

The elven slave, with chains tattooed across her brow, hovered over the dying Shadow fae, wringing her hands. Her gaze shifted from Bleakhart, the sorcerer, to the empress's engorged stomach.

"The babes will not be born alive. I have done everything I can." The elf spoke in a whisper that would not have been heard had the room not grown so silent and somber. The sconces on the walls guttered with each belabored moan of the empress.

Bleakhart leaned in close to the slave and hissed, "I know you have ways. I will unbind you if you use your magic to save them."

The elf's eyes widened, her expression shifting from hope to terror as she realized what the sorcerer was asking of her. No elemental magic, not even elven, would pry the children from her womb, and Bleakhart knew it. Only old magic, forbidden for centuries by her people.

Before the elf could respond, Empress Alize bolted upright. The blood vessels burst in her eyes as her gaze connected with the slave's, the sclera gone red, pupils dilated, swallowing the violet irises.

"Get them out of me. Please, I beg of you!" The once proud ruler known for never bowing sounded broken, her voice hoarse from long hours of screaming.

"My lady, I cannot–" the slave started, but the Alize reached out and wrapped her hands around the elf's slender throat, causing her to choke on her words.

"Make sure one of the children lives. There must be an heir. Call them Ereda and Lorna." The two names fell from the mother's lips, forced out moments before consciousness left her. She fell back, her body spent, her head hitting the stone with a dull thud before the slave could regain her strangled breath.

The elf turned wild, terrified eyes to Bleakhart as she massaged the bruises forming on her throat. Her mouth worked, but no words came out.

The sorcerer leaned in so close that his spittle flew in the elf's face as he shouted, "I do not care what your people forbid! You belong to us now. Your people are on the wrong side of history—soon to be dead and gone. So you'll do as I say. Get them out of her. Now. Or, so help me, I'll kill you and every other elf held in the dungeons."

The slave pressed her lips into a grim line. "It will kill her to bring them into the world. You know elven magic cannot do such things. It requires blood magic. Old magic. Terrifying. The cost will be the mother's life. Possibly more. Blood magic can alter destinies for generations."

Bleakhart snorted and waved his hand at the empress lying motionless on the slab. Her skin faded to the gray of stone, mouth agape, wings hanging limp, shedding pale feathers that were once black to the floor. Her chest barely rose and fell as she wheezed.

"Do not speak to me of destiny," Bleakhart spat, "if you could read the stars as you claim, if your people truly knew what was to be, you would not be where you are today. And look"—he gestured at the stone tablet that had birthed three generations of empresses—" she is already as good as gone. It is too late for her."

The slave studied Alize. The empress's life force ebbed. There was barely enough magic left to sustain her. She nodded. "It is so."

"So do it."

Bleakhart grasped the elf's wrist and, with a spell, removed the shackles around them. They fell to the floor with a clatter. "Don't try anything, elf." The sorcerer glanced at the shadow guards standing by the door. They moved forward, menacing, to ring the stone table.

Bleakhart thrust a dagger at the elf. The slave's hands shook as she raised the athame above her head, then brought it down violently. She slashed the blade across the empress's wrist and continued across her own before pressing the wounds together. Her eyelids fluttered, eyes rolling back in her head, revealing only the milky whites. She whispered words in an ancient, sibilant tongue. Her red blood and the empress's black mingled, spilling down her arms. It pooled in her hands as, with a shriek and a final heroic feat of dark magic, the twins were brought into the world.

A deluge of blood and a thick cloud of shadows poured from the spasming body of the empress as the last of her magic abandoned her—a single sigh, a final breath, separated the girls who sprang from the dying shadow fae's loins. First, a pale gray creature with snakes of black hair forming a crown around a face the color of the moons: Ereda - the one who would rule.

Then, almost as an afterthought, the traitor was born. Lavender-eyed and silent, dark like her mother, but with no violence in her gaze, only quiet contemplation.

The silence left in the wake of their expulsion from the womb into the world was more disarming than any scream. It lasted only a moment before the firstborn shattered it with her cries. Ereda's shrieks set the slave's nerves on edge. She ground her teeth as she plucked the child from the bloodied stone and thrust her at the Shadow fae milkmaid, who set her to suckle her breast in the hopes of silencing the infant. But when the child's sharp teeth clamped on her teat, the nursemaid's screams picked up where the mother's and daughter's had left off.

The second daughter, Lorna, remained as motionless as the dead thing that had once been the empress. But unlike her mother, the child was alive, only possessed of a profound, uncanny stillness near as unnerving as the tempest that was her sister. No servant came to her, for she was of no importance. She was a second-born child— a cursed thing that had stolen the proud empress's life.

The birth of one child was rare enough. Unlike the elves, fae wombs were not fast to quicken, and deliveries were always difficult. But two babes? Even a creature as powerful as the Shadow empress could not survive the labor of twin babies. If Lorna had not shared her womb with Ereda, the empress might still be. And she would be reminded of that for all her days.

Bleakhart gazed down at the ruined body of the woman who had ruled the Shadow fae for millennia. Her hair had turned bone-white, her skin was paper-thin, and no breath stirred within her chest. Empress Alize Blackburn was no more.

How strange, he thought, *that such small creatures could bring the end of an era in their wake. A woman who invaded a foreign world, laid elven cities to waste, claimed them as her own, and enslaved countless minions could be unmade by two mewling babies who know not what they do.*

"Sir," said a familiar voice. The father stood in the doorway. Once king consort, but now that his lover was dead meat and bone with no magic in her anymore, a nobody. He would hold no position at court with Alize dead. The babes would be raised by advisors. It was the way of the shadow fae.

"She is gone," Bleakhart informed the man.

The sorcerer ignored the man's choked sobs and studied the children who had wrought this catastrophe.

Tears flowed freely down the milkmaid's face just as blood ran down her breast as the firstborn tore into her flesh. The other still lay on the marble birthing bed turned funeral pyre—silent, patient, waiting her turn.

As if she knows her place already, Bleakhart thought. "This one," he pointed towards the babe at the breast, "is Ereda. A new empress is born. That one"—he shifted his gaze back to the other—"Lorna. The Shadow's sister."

"May I hold them?" the consort asked, his eyes haunted, for surely he knew he would never see the children again after this.

"That one, fine," Bleakhart grumbled, indicating the still-silent Lorna lying on the slab. "Then find some slut to nurse the whelp when you're done coddling her." He turned to the armored guards, motionless as statues securing the chamber doors. "And kill the elf. She failed in her duties."

"My Lord, I tried. I saved the babes. I—" The slave collapsed to her knees, pressing her face to Bleakhart's feet to kiss them in a desperate show of reverence as she begged for mercy.

The sorcerer gave her a swift kick for her efforts and barked, "You failed! Alize is dead."

Bleakhart turned away, suddenly sickened by the scene before him. "Make the necessary arrangements for a coronation," he ordered the scribes, who sat with pen in hand, documenting the tragedy that had occurred this day.

Sibling Rivalry

One Hundred Years Later

The river Nyx ran as red as elven blood down from the Funeral Mountains, where it was diverted into the crimson moat that swirled around Castle Bleak. A small stream flowed from the trench into the castle proper, coming to a terminus at a large pool in the central courtyard.

One of Lorna Blackburn's first memories was being held face down in this pool, with her sister's claw-like hands digging into her shoulders as she plunged Lorna beneath the surface, again and again. She could still taste the mingled copper and sulfur flavor of the water.

Now, she watched children splash, the water shimmering like oil slicks on their black and gray skin, wondering why she and Ereda had never played so innocently together. Why was there always malice between them? Why not the laughter and love that ought to be shared between two motherless girls?

Lorna knew the answer. Because Ereda would never forgive her. She was cursed. A second daughter, unwanted, who had stolen from Ereda and from the Shadow court, their mother, the empress. With a sigh, she set these thoughts aside. There was nothing she could do about them. Ereda was what she was; everything Lorna was not, and that was unlikely to change. Surely, in all the Ethereal Realms, no twin sisters had ever been born less alike.

Lorna glanced down at the leather-bound book that lay open in her lap, eyes skimming the perfectly even lines of elegant script. She squinted, trying to decipher the elven verse. Her translations had come a long way over the years, but much of the text's meaning was still lost on her. She ran her fingers over the dry, fragile page, wishing she could absorb the words—and their magic—with a touch, as it was said the elves could do.

"What I wouldn't give to have those soft fingers caressing my–"

Lorna stiffened, and her leathery bat-like wings flared behind her as she jerked her head up. She curled her fingers, tendrils of black smoke rising from the tips, ready to attack. Then seeing who it was, scoffed and relaxed her fist. Osiris Bane's smirking countenance loomed over her. His eyes glittered, deep violet and full of mischief.

He stood with arms folded across his chest, gazing down with an air of superiority he, a mere emissary—had no right to possess. His black feathered wings shadowed Lorna, the unruly mass of his ebony curls tumbling across his forehead, and a little buzz of something, irritation or excitement—perhaps both—filled Lorna. She tamped down the latter of the emotions and got to her feet. Even then, Osiris stood more than a full head taller than her, just like her sister.

"Only a fool sneaks up on a Blackburn, Osiris," Lorna admonished as the last tendrils of smoke drifted away.

Osiris's earnest expression didn't waver when he said, "If I am a fool, it is only because your beauty renders me one, my lady." His lip curled up on one side, revealing a sharp, white canine.

Lorna was torn between slapping the smug look off his face and pulling him into a passionate kiss. Neither response was appropriate, so instead, she sighed and asked, "Why are you here, Osiris? Can I not get a moment's peace?"

Osiris dramatically brought his hand to his heart as if wounded by Lorna's words. "Is it so far-fetched that I might simply want to bask in the beauty of the Shadow's sister?"

"Yes," Lorna deadpanned. "And stop calling me that. How many times do I have to say it?" She loathed that moniker, and he knew it.

The feigned hurt look passed, giving way to Osiris's characteristic smirk. "You know me too well, my beautiful dark heart. I come at your sister's bidding. She requests your presence in the war room."

Lorna grunted. She should have known. Ereda thought of little else of late besides the war

she was plotting. Lorna had no interest in her sister's plans to dominate the Ethereal Realms and subjugate the elves and anyone else who stood in her way. She preferred solitude outside with a book to the oppressive constraints of the over-embellished war room full of pompous know-it-alls who—

"Shall I escort you?" Osiris interrupted her thoughts, lifting his arm so she could slip her hand into the crook of it.

Lorna sniffed and kept her hands exactly where they were, at her sides. "No need." She was already striding away as she spoke.

"Must you be so cold, Lorna Blackburn? There must be something I can do to win your heart," Osiris called after her.

"You're an errand boy without a drop of noble blood in you, Osiris Bane. And you're an arrogant rogue to boot—" She would have gone on had Osiris not interrupted her again.

"You know your sister doesn't want a noble match for you. Too much threat to the succession. And we complement one another perfectly. You're the brains, and I'm the brawn. You're the lace, and I'm the lea–"

Lorna didn't slow her pace as she climbed the stone stairs that led inside the castle, interrupting him to shout, "More like oil and water, Osiris. The two never mix."

"You'll change your mind one day. You'll see." He said it like a challenge that carried across the growing space between them.

Lorna paused on the landing, then turned to face him. "You like to call me the Shadow's sister, but you'd do well to remember who I am. With a word to Ereda, I can have you sent to her dungeons as fodder for Bleakheart's next experiment with elven magic."

A broad grin spread across Osiris's face. "But you never would."

And the frustrating thing was, he was right.

Lorna stepped into the war room and immediately regretted it. She tried to ignore the claustrophobia she felt when confined within the tapestry-draped walls. Images of shadow fae mounted on nightmare steeds converged on screaming mutilated elves. She never understood why only the massacres and the destruction were immortalized for eternity.

"It took you long enough," Ereda snarled.

Lorna's eyes were drawn away from the wall hangings toward her sister. Ereda sat with her back straight and stiff as a board at the head of the long, stone table, thin lips pursed in dismay. Her gray hair was in a tangled nest around her wan face. Coils of snakes slithered out occasionally to lap at the air with red forked tongues. Though the Shadow empress was not beautiful, she radiated an aura of power that was difficult not to be cowed by.

Lorna dipped into a low curtsy, bowing her head and hiding her chagrined expression behind the curtain of her long violet hair. "My apologies, Your Majesty. I wasn't aware we had a meeting this afternoon. I was out getting some air."

Ereda snorted and rolled her eyes heavenward. "You and your air. Perhaps you're better suited for the Court of Sky than Shadows. Shall I ship you off and let the Sky fae have their way with you, sister? I could trade you for Uncle Emerett. He's been in their dungeon for an age."

An idle threat, Lorna knew. Ereda would never put a shadow sorceress of her aptitude in the hands of a court that openly opposed her designs. Not even as a prisoner. Of course, the Court of Sky wasn't known for its heavy-handed tactics. They probably fed their captives bread and honey. But it was a risk and not one worth taking. The way her sister tossed out threats with so little regard made Lorna bristle, but she forced a smile and sunk even lower in her curtsy.

"My place is by your side, sister." The statement lacked conviction, but the empress did not appear to notice.

"Yes, yes. Well, sit down in your already, then. We have important things to discuss."

Lorna took one of the empty seats at the table. It was a small group of the usual suspects. Her two head generals, Drake and Tyran, who could never agree, sat across from one another. At least they wouldn't be shouting from across the room, though the risk of one or the other being injured in a brawl increased in this circumstance. Lorna wouldn't be surprised to see them bicker over which end of a sword to hold.

Beside General Blake sat Master Bleakhart. The pale

and trembling wisp of a man was a half-breed—his shadow blood tainted with that of the fire fae. Most mistrusted him, but Ereda had taken a liking to him—specifically to his techniques for torturing secrets from the captive elves—and she could not be warned away from him by her other advisors. Apparently, he was a sorcerer of great renown. It was even said his magic had brought them both into the world. However, there were whispers that something else entirely had spared the twins and killed their mother. Either way, Ereda had entrusted experimentation to his frail, shaking hands.

Bleakhart looked up, and Lorna quickly averted her eyes, though not in time to avoid catching his creepy milky-white gaze. She didn't like Bleakhart, not because of his mixed heritage, but because she could sense his cruelty. It seemed to ebb out of him along with the heat that leaked from his body.

And she had heard the anguished screams of the elves kept in the dungeons.

Ereda cleared her throat, and everyone in the room snapped to attention. "I suppose you're wondering why I've summoned you four and not the others," the Shadow empress began, which was true, particularly for Lorna. Ereda was displeased with the rate of Lorna's progress on the elven manuscripts she'd been tasked with interpreting into shadow tongue. This strained their already tenuous relationship, and Lorna had been invited to fewer meetings of late. Not that she minded. These meetings were a formality Lorna would just as soon avoid entirely.

"I'm sure her Majesty has—"

Bleakhart's soft voice was silenced by a glare from the empress. "I don't need your flattery, half-breed," Ereda snapped, bringing her fingers to her temples and massaging as if dealing with her advisors represented the pinnacle of tedium. "As I was saying. You four have special roles to play in what will become our greatest conquest."

Lorna bit back a scoff and examined her fingernails. They had been at war with the elves for some time now, and she had seen no signs of an imminent victory. The native species of the Ethereal Realms had more powerful magic, greater knowledge, and they formed a united front. The fae were divided, their loyalty bound to their birth courts, and their armies spread across the Realms many miles apart. Some, like the Dreamers and the Sky fae, did not seek conquest at all but instead a peaceful coexistence with the elves.

"Lorna"—Ereda's eyes, steel gray and hard as flint, cut to her sister—"I'm reassigning you."

"But..." Lorna bit back her protest as a plume of shadows began to swirl around Ereda. The Shadow empress disliked being interrupted.

"Those translations are taking too long. It's been years, and all we have are a few disjointed phrases. Useless. We are going to try it my way now." Ereda's gaze shifted from Lorna to Bleakhart. "She's to work under you, Bleakhart, who I'm equally disappointed in. Where is my undead army? Where are the soldiers you promised me?"

The empress let out a long, drawn-out sigh. "Perhaps the two of you useless fools working together will be able to accomplish something, hmm? If Bleakhart can't torture the secrets out of the elves, maybe my sweet little sister can cajole them with that silver tongue of hers. "

Lorna fought to maintain a neutral expression. Her tongue was no more silver than Ereda's heart was gold. She preferred not to speak at all, truth be told, let alone try to coerce slaves and captives to part with their secrets. She was also less than thrilled with the prospect of being stationed alongside the old mongrel sorcerer in the dungeons. She loved her work with the ancient texts and was making headway. Just not fast enough for her ever-impatient sister, apparently.

But once Ereda had made her mind up, there was no changing it, so there was no point in protesting.

Bleakhart looked no more pleased by this turn of events than Lorna did. His thin lips were drawn down into a quivering frown, and he worried the amulet he wore around his neck with knobby fingers, eyebrows furrowed.

"Well? What are you waiting for?" Ereda's eyes shifted from Bleakhart to Lorna, then back again. "Get to work. You're dismissed." She clapped her hands, the sound of her many rings knocking together cutting through the silence in the room.

Being dismissed from the meeting while the generals remained was a slap in the face. It seemed both Lorna and Bleakhart had found themselves on the wrong side of the empress's favor. The disgraced pair rose, bowed, and left the throne room, Lorna leading the way.

She walked quickly, attempting to slip away without further discussion, but despite his advanced age and fragile physique, Bleakhart managed to match her pace.

"I don't see you often in the dungeons, girl," the half-fire fae commented.

Lorna paused in her steps and turned to face the sorcerer. "That is because I dislike the dungeons just as I dislike you." She spoke softly as she always did but gave him a hard stare, hoping he would scamper back into his lair and leave her be.

Unfortunately, Bleakhart seemed unfazed by her disdain and went on. "Do you know, when the fae first set foot in the Ethereal Realms, there was no castle, no courtyards? There was only the palace beneath the earth. It was built first, long before—"

Lorna sighed and cut him off. "Yes, and then my great-grandmother set about capturing the elves and stealing their magic, and slowly the Shadow fae returned to the surface to claim our empire. And over time, we pushed the elves back to the Heart of the Forest, where the Dream Fae assimilated with them, but they have been a thorn in our side ever since. I do not need a history lesson, Bleakhart."

Bleakhart coughed with a wet mucousy sound and reached out to grab Lorna's hand. His fingers were uncomfortably warm on her skin, the product of the mingled fire fae blood in his veins.

"You'll be spending a good bit of time in the dungeons with me now, girl. Best get used to the shadows you've been shunning your whole life. I'll see you tomorrow at raven's hour."

Lorna tugged her hand away from him and wheeled on her heel, heading for her chambers in the upper tower. Only when she was out of Bleakhart's sight did she rub the burn marks on her flesh left by his touch, cursing her sister under her breath.

The Undercity

The following morning dawned dreary as ever over Castle Bleak. Thin rays of sunlight filtered through the dense, dark cloud cover, barely bright enough to stream through Lorna's window. A thick manuscript about the history of the Court of Earth that she'd been reading the previous evening still lay open on the pillow beside her. She gazed longingly at it, wishing she could bring it down to the red pool where the children played to study unmolested.

But she knew that wasn't an option. Not when she was expected down in the dungeons with Bleakhart to aid in his experiments. The very idea of the dank under-city and the old sorcerous goat made her shudder, but there was no help for it. Ereda had ordered it, and so it would be.

Lorna went over to the small, gilded black mirror and

stared at her reflection as she combed out her long dark hair, which shimmered almost violet in the weak morning light. Everyone said she resembled her mother with her indigo gem-shaped eyes, bat-like wings shot through with gold, and gleaming onyx skin. But Lorna had seen the paintings, and she saw only the barest resemblance on the surface. The features might be there, but all the renderings of Alize Blackburn portrayed a proud woman, straight-backed like Ereda, eyes shining with purpose and cool calculation. No, Lorna was convinced she could be nothing like the dead Shadow empress, but she wished she'd had a chance to meet her and her exiled father.

Sharp rapping on her chamber door drew Lorna's eyes away from the reflection in the mirror, and she scowled at the interruption. She ignored it long enough to set the brush down and pull on a pair of black buskins and the same flowing back and gold robes she wore daily. The banging increased in its insistence.

"What is it?" she demanded as she flung the door open to find herself face-to-face with *him*.

Osiris Bane leaned against the doorframe, his black crow's wings blocking her egress, his usual playful yet judgemental smile painted on his irritatingly handsome face.

"You again?" Lorna moved to slam the door in his face, but Osiris blocked the motion with his booted foot.

"Your sister–" he started, but she rolled her eyes and cut him off.

"Sent you, I know, errand boy. Why?"

"You know, Lorna, you could be kinder to me. I

think I'm the only person in this castle who actually likes you," Osiris teased.

Some of the bitterness leaked from Lorna's scowl with those words. It was true. Everyone else in Castle Bleak either ignored her or went out of their way to torment the strange, quiet sister of the empress, whose nose was always buried in a book and who craved sunlight while the others clung to the shadows.

"I apologize, Osiris. I've only just woken up, and I have to get down to those horrid dungeons and that awful sorcerer. I'm not in the best mood. What does my sweet sister want of me now?" Lorna tried again in a milder tone.

Osiris's jovial grin slipped into a smirk. "She thinks you might have forgotten how to get around in the dungeons; it's been so long since you've been down in your ancestral holdfast. I'm to escort you, so you don't lose your way."

Truth be told, Lorna wasn't sure she did recall how to navigate the layer upon layer of twisting tunnels that comprised the small city beneath the castle, but that didn't make Ereda sending an escort—as if she was a helpless child—any less irritating. Lorna looked for something to throw, but there was nothing in reach, so instead, she batted at him with her hand. Osiris caught her by the wrist and pulled her closer to him.

"Don't kill the messenger." He let out a bark of laughter and tousled her hair, just like he'd done when they were children, then released her and took a step back, so his wings no longer blocked the doorway. "Are you ready to go?"

Tendrils of smoky Shadow streamed off Lorna as she fought to contain her magic and her... what? What was she feeling just then? It wasn't anger. Well, maybe somewhat, but also something else. She didn't have time to puzzle it out. Instead, she pushed past Osiris and out into the hall, storming towards the stairwell.

Osiris followed; Lorna could hear his footsteps behind her. She wasn't sure if she was relieved or angry.

They descended for what felt like an eternity, Lorna leading the way, straight down into the bowels of the catacombs, Osiris close behind, his footsteps in a rhythm with her own. The walls were claustrophobic, with occasional blue flame torches studding them.

Neither Lorna nor Osiris needed the light to see—Shadow fae were one with the darkness. It fed their magic. No, the torches weren't for them. A dead elf could spill no secrets, and too many fell, making the long trek down. Immortality only lasted as long as the body containing it remained intact, whether fae or elf. A broken body was no fit vessel, and physical trauma could cause it to abandon the bearer, dissipating into the Void, leaving behind only an empty shell.

Still, Lorna was glad for the blue flames. Though it was a part of her, the impenetrable darkness of the undercity weighed more heavily the deeper they went; perfectly cold, utterly indifferent. It reminded her of her sister.

The screams started softly at first, and Lorna couldn't be sure whether she had imagined them, conjured them up in her mind. Were the cries a psychosomatic response to the oppressive tightness of the stairwell walls closing in on her, narrowing as they traveled deeper? A product of her mind protesting against the descent into a nightmarish place she had spent most of her life trying to avoid?

They reached the bottom of the staircase, where a cavernous, circular room swelled before them. The crypt. She'd been brought here for lessons as a girl, and the memories it brought back were not fond ones. Black and gold tapestries, moldering, some as old as the undercity itself, lined the walls. Statues of Shadow empresses past, hewn from gleaming black volcanic rock, were erected on the far wall, votives glowing before each of them.

Lorna tracked her ancestors until her eye snagged on the carved figure of her mother, Alize Blackburn. Her gaze briefly lingered there, trying to find some likeness to herself in the vessel dedicated to her mother. But then a plea, broken and strangled, desperate in the strange, lilting tongue of the elves, sounded. Closer now. Real, and certainly not in her head.

Lorna reached out unconsciously and grasped Osiris's forearm. She clamped her fingers tightly around it, clinging to the solidity of his flesh. He cleared his throat slightly and patted her on the head. "I see Ereda was right. It has been a while since you've ventured down here."

Lorn turned to face him and found his usual mocking grin replaced by sympathy that etched tiny lines around his downturned lips. Lorna turned away, uncomfortable with his attention. But Osiris drew her back, cupping her face in his hand, causing her to meet his stormy ebony eyes.

In a hushed tone, he said, "You're too gentle for this

court, Lorna, but you'll have to live with it. You're the Shadow's sister, and there is no other place for you but under Ereda's yoke. This is going to be hard, and you will not enjoy it. But it's the burden you carry. Bend, don't break."

Lorna tried to hide her surprise at his words. In all the long years she'd known Osiris Bane, she had never seen him so solemn. There was always a jibe, always teasing and taunting. Unsure what else to do, she lifted her chin, nodding to him.

"Of course. It is my duty. Lead the way. Let us see what fresh hell my sister has cursed me with now," Lorna said, forcing the words out past the swell of fear in her throat.

He gave her a wistful smile. "If you'd let go of me... I'm afraid I'll lose circulation in my arm soon." With that, the spell was broken, the moment gone, Osiris back to his usual antics.

Lorna blushed furiously and relinquished her white-knuckle grasp on her escort's arm, murmuring an apology, and Osiris returned to the business at hand. He strode towards a gated opening on the left side of the chamber, Lorna behind him, dragging her feet as she went.

"The key." Osiris held a large black metal key forged in the shape of a serpent, jaws open wide. "Ereda asked me to give it to you."

Lorna gripped the key with trembling fingers and inserted it into the lock. The tumbler's rumble sounded like breaking bones and echoed off the stone walls until it was drowned out by another distant shriek. She pushed the door, which opened with a scream of hinges, then slipped the key into her robes.

For a moment, she only stood there, sucking down deep breaths of the dank air, fetid with staleness, tart with candle wax.

"Come along," Osiris encouraged, jerking his head towards the gate. He passed through it, out of the crypt, and into more winding corridors.

Lorna followed a few feet behind. She felt a vague sense of familiarity as they passed several tunnels leading in different directions. Osiris turned left and led her down a narrower passageway. They walked together for some time, often turning down tributaries, the undercity such a maze that Lorna was glad Ereda had sent Osiris as a guide despite her initial frustration.

The silence in the tunnels was eerie. No sound except for their footsteps on stone and the soft plunk of water dripping from the tunnel walls. The quiet was occasionally punctuated by screams, each making Lorna flinch involuntarily.

Ahead, the corridor abruptly ended, their way barred by a heavy metal door. Osiris stopped and moved to the side, gesturing for Lorna to go first. "This is as far as I'm permitted to go. Will you be able to make your way back?" He sounded earnest, and his brow furrowed, shadowing his eyes in the blue torchlight.

Lorna forced herself to scoff and say, "Of course," with far more conviction than she felt.

Osiris reached over and took her hand so suddenly

that it caused her to start, then leaned in close, brushing her violet hair aside to whisper in her ear. "Do whatever he tells you to do, Lorna. I know what you are, but you'll have to pretend to be something else. Ereda will..."

"Is that the Shadow's sister out there?" Bleakhart's voice wavered from behind the door, cutting Osiris off.

Lorna wished he could have finished. Ereda what? Why had her sister banished her to this dark lair? Did he know her intentions? Or was it just speculation? But Osiris released her hand, dipped into a bow, and then pulled the surrounding shadows to him, cloaking himself and disappearing. Leaving Lorna staring at the closed door.

When it opened, Bleakhart appeared, backlit by ferocious red torches, the likes of which one never saw in the Shadow court. His eyes burned like simmering embers as he stared at her. Slight and hunched as the sorcerer was, he still towered over Lorna's petite frame, and she found herself shrinking away from him as he stepped toward her.

"Lorna," he acknowledged with a stiff nod, sounding no more pleased about Lorna being there than she was.

"Bleakhart." She raised her chin and stepped through the open door, entering the true heart of the dungeon.

Bleakhart didn't speak. Instead, he beckoned with a wave of his hand and began walking, leading Lorna down another narrow tunnel, then into a room, which she presumed served as his office. A black stone slab was positioned in the center, with a single, terribly uncomfortable-looking stone seat. Bleakhart lowered himself into it, leaving her standing awkwardly across from him.

She fidgeted, twisting the fabric of her robes between her fingers. Bleakhart stared down at her as if she were a curiosity, something distasteful but interesting. "You speak their tongue?" he finally asked her, apparently of a mind that no further pleasantries needed to be exchanged between them.

It took a moment for Lorna's flustered mind to make sense of the question, but another distant scream in the elven tongue hammered his point home. She raised a shoulder in a shrug. "I've never actually spoken elven. I've only translated it from scrolls and manuscripts. And I do not know the meaning of every word. Only some." She paused. "Just a few, really."

Bleakhart snorted and rolled his eyes. "So you read... or attempted to read, a few books. A lot of good that does me."

Lorna stared at the floor, working her fingers even faster as her agitation mounted. What was she doing here? She hated the underground city more than anywhere else in the Realms. And while Lorna had always known her sister was driven to achieve the results she wanted, she never imagined Ereda could be cruel enough to subject her to something like this.

The old half-fire fae seemed either not to notice or care about her discomfort. Bleakhart sighed, then coughed. "Do you even know what we are doing down here? What our work is?" He raised a bushy copper-colored brow, his lips pressed together in disapproval.

Lorna shook her head, and Bleakhart grunted in apparent annoyance, then went on to explain. "The elves have magic much stronger than ours, and that's how they've held back our attempts to destroy them, or at the very least drive them out of the realms, to the wild lands in the south, as we did the mortals centuries ago."

Lorna shot him a withering look. Everyone knew that. Did he think she was a child? The mortals had been no match for the fae. They were weak, with short life spans, and though they propagated quickly, they were all so afraid of dying that one glimpse of a fae army on the march had been enough to send them packing, driving them into the uninhabited wilderness in the south. They were lucky their race had survived at all. If Nimione, the ruler of the Court of Sea, hadn't agreed with the sky fae and the dream fae that they were no threat, they would have been done for. Her mother and Asheron Drogon, ruler of the Fire Court, would have systematically eradicated them as Ereda was attempting to do to the elves.

But Ereda couldn't be free from the plague that was the elves. Because they were too powerful.

"I know the histories quite well, old man," Lorna retorted.

Bleakhart's lip curled into a smirk, revealing yellowed teeth. "Do you, though? You know the elves have mastered all the spheres of power, unlike we fae born to wield but a single sphere based on our bloodline. We have tried cross-breeding in an attempt to gain such control."

He paused, a bitter expression etching itself into his features that made Lorna wonder, was he, with his half-fire and half-shadow blood, perhaps, one such experiment?

Before she could inquire about it, he rushed on. "But the results proved that it only splits the difference. Those born of the blood of two courts can use schools of magic, yes, but the power? The control?" He waved his hand in the air dismissively. "Halved. And the more you dilute a bloodline, the weaker the magic becomes. Mongrels mated with other mixed-bloods might as well have been born mortals for all the spells they could weave."

As Lorna mulled over the sorcerer's words in the brief pause that hung in the air between them, Ereda's ultimate goal clicked in her mind. Her eyes widened and shot up from the cracked stone floor to meet Bleakhart's. "So you're trying to discover how the elves can wield all the spheres without the diminishing returns caused by our...breeding experiments?" she surmised.

Bleakhart cocked his head to the side and tilted his hand in a so-so gesture. "That, and other things. Older magic, the magic that brought you and your sister into the world but killed your mother."

The old magic... The air in the room suddenly felt heavy and too warm. Beads of sweat broke out on Lorna's brow, and she wished there was somewhere to sit down, as the words felt like a punch in her gut. Instead, she leaned against the table, trying to appear casual as her mind whirled. She had read about the old magic. Though the writings had been ancient and among the most difficult to decipher, she knew from her studies that it was terrible in nature. It involved black works of spellcraft and curses that relied on blood, banned by the elves eons ago, long before the fae had set foot in the Ethereal Realms. But the elves were an ancient people. Did they still know the secrets to such magic? And the idea that it had been used on her mother... and that Ereda was seeking to control it...

"Are you all right, girl? You look as though you've seen a ghost." Bleakhart shattered Lorna's trance.

She nodded mutely, unable to find her voice. Bleakhart continued. "So, that is what we must do, you and I. Break the elves, and learn the core of their magics, both old and new. And if we do not do it soon, I fear your sister..."

He went on, but Lorna wasn't listening. She already knew what her sister did to those who failed her. Their heads were mounted on pikes, decorating the walls of the upper castle for all to see.

Bleakhart rose when he was finished speaking and tottered to the door that led back to the dungeon proper.

"So I assume," he said, "you're ready to get started?"

Lorna knew in her soul she wasn't. She simply wasn't built for this.

But she had no choice.

The Prophecy

T he darkness was uncomfortable, but Lorna soon grew accustomed to it as her ancestors once had when they were forced beneath the surface for survival—through necessity.

It was amazing how quickly one could adapt. Lorna wondered if the Shadow fae's time underground had made their society what it was today—cold, detached, focused on survival, conquest, and the never-ending reach for *more*. More power, more land, more control. They had charged straight for the heart of the elven empire when they invaded the Realms and suffered more for it than any other court. Was the thirst for domination just a bred desire for revenge? Or a desperate drive to never be forced so low again?

She brushed the thoughts aside. The elders were lost. There was no one to answer her questions, but she felt the call of the darkness in her blood down there in the deepest depths. She felt the pull of the shadows. They caressed her and beckoned for her to use them, to claim their power. And as the screams grew louder, echoing otherworldly eeriness, she felt the urge to pull the shadows to her, cloak herself in them, and flee.

But she resisted, keeping her eyes on Bleakhart, who walked ahead, focusing on his shuffling footsteps. He stopped in front of a room walled off by metal bars and said, "Here we are. I suggest you prepare yourself. It isn't pretty in there."

Lorna swallowed hard and took a tentative step forward. The cell was pitch black, darker than anything she'd ever seen. Magic, she knew. Only shadow magic could render a darkness so complete. Lorna whispered a spell, and her pupils flared wide, brightening her vision, illuminating a sight she would forever wish she could forget.

Shackled to the walls, radiating their telltale glow, at least a dozen elves were bound, the chains siphoning their magic down to an ebb—enough to keep them alive, but only barely.

Elves were traditionally tall and slender with luminescent skin in various hues tattooed with power runes. These specimens were emaciated, bones jutting at odds angles beneath dull graying complexions, their runes blackened from decay and disuse, flesh marred by shadow burns.

Lorna's eyes lingered on the runes. How many times had she studied them in the tomes pillaged from elven libraries? And now, an opportunity to get the answers she'd sought all her life... but all she felt was revulsion. Lorna looked away, her stomach knotting. She was sure she would have lost its contents if it weren't empty. As it was, she swallowed a gag.

Then Bleakhart's spindly fingers were on her face, pinching her chin as he drew her gaze up to meet his. "Your sister wants answers, and that is what we get for her," he began, then paused, his jaw working as if carefully considering his words. "I won't ask you to beat their secrets out of them. That is my job," he went on, with the quickest flash of a grimace that made Lorna wonder if he, too, found this whole business distasteful. "Perhaps you could try to—"

"Talk with them? In their own language?" Lorna suggested, unable to bite back a bitter laugh. How many years of torturing them, taking them apart, and studying their insides... and no one had ever tried asking them? She forced herself to tamp her frustration and said, "Let me inside."

There was no lock to release. The gates were sealed with shadow magic, and with a muttered word and a quick wave of Bleakhart's gnarled hand, the bars parted enough to allow Lorna to step through, then sealed behind her just as quickly.

Her eyes trailed over the elves. Their eyes were dull, hollow, sunken in their sockets, and she felt a pang of pity. Whatever the elves had done to her ancestors, no one deserved this. They had only been protecting their homeland. She shook her head to silence the thoughts. She could not afford to feel sorry for them now; it would break her.

Lorna took a few tentative steps towards the wretched being nearest her. It was a female with hair that had likely once been emerald, now the color of moss. Her pale green skin was pulled taut across high cheekbones.

The elf's eyes were closed and were it not for the shallow rise and fall of her chest, Lorna might have thought there was no life left in her. She lowered herself to her knees, what she deemed a safe distance away. They were shackled, yes, and weak, but she knew elves were dangerous. There had been rebellions before. Ill-fated, but she had seen what a handful of slaves could do with even meager powers if one wasn't careful.

"Acquata a amsir," Lorna tried the words she had only read up to now, tasting the elven on her tongue. It sounded nothing like the lilting cadence it ought to have but was apparently close enough. The captive opened her eyes to milky slits at the sound of her own language.

"Amsa Coralline," the elf responded, surprising Lorna by giving over her name so readily. But then, the elves did not guard their names against their enemies as the fae did.

"Shaksa common?" Lorna tried, hoping the elf spoke the tongue shared by all the fae courts.

The elf gave a faint nod and then said, "Some."

Lorna breathed a sigh of relief as she'd reached about the extent that her translational Elven could carry her in a dialogue. She opened her mouth to ask another question, but before she got the words out, the elf let out a sudden gasp, her eyes going wide.

"You," she whispered. "You're touched by prophecy. The dark star who will deliver the Legion Queen."

Lorna started and pulled farther away as the captive leaned forward, baring her broken teeth in a smile or a grimace; she wasn't entirely sure which.

They stared at each other for a moment, and Lorna's

mind whirled. Prophecy. The key tool of the elven astrologers was just one of many weapons they wielded that the fae could not grasp. The ability to divine from the stars, but more, once those threads of the future were revealed, to follow them. Like strands of spider silk in a web, those who read the star charts could, it was said, see the halos of destiny worn by those fate-touched.

But destiny was terrifying; it caught you in your grip and would never release. Destiny changed everything. Did Lorna, who lived in such solitary misery, truly want to know what the fates had in store for her?

No. So, Lorna leaped to her feet and made to bolt for the door. She would not be a slave to prophesy. Would not have her future driven by the words of this elven slave. Would not—

The slave reached out again. "Stay. You cannot tell me you're not curious."

Lorna flinched but didn't run. She stayed, turning around slowly to face the elven woman again. Despite her palpable terror at the idea of being a pawn in some grand, unfathomable scheme, the slave was right. She was curious.

"You are the Shadow's Sister," the elf went on in heavily accented Common.

Lorna balked at the sound of the hated name and would have turned away again if something in the elf's eyes didn't hold her.

This is why they're dangerous, she reminded herself. *This could all be a ruse, a lie to cause distraction before exacting revenge. But no, don't be foolish. They're in chains, their magic bound. Keep your distance, and they cannot harm you.*

She cleared her throat and reproached, "My name is Lorna. Not the Shadow's sister."

The elf raised her shoulders in a shrug. "A name is nothing but a tether to destiny. You can choose whatever name you wish, but a name is written in the stars, and yours is the Shadow's sister. I can show you." She reached out with a skeletal hand, bruised, paper-thin skin covering her bones, and whispered, "I can reveal the prophecy."

For a moment, Lorna was perfectly still, staring at the floor. She could sense eyes on her, not just this elf's filmy white gaze. Others around the room were staring at her too. A hundred of them, it felt like. She released a ragged sigh and raised her arm slowly, reaching for the slave. With their fingers mere inches apart, she exhaled a shaky breath, and then they touched.

A sensation Lorna could not describe shot through her. It was as if something burned her from within, a lightning bolt that began at the base of her skull, scorching down every vertebra in her spine. She fell face first, her knees cracking against the stone floor, her head following.

But Lorna barely felt the pain, only a dull tingle as if she were removed, as far away as the voice calling out her name. She tried to open her mouth to cry out and lift herself from where she'd fallen, but her body felt paralyzed—no... disconnected. She was floating. And then she was disappearing.

The stars. A million stars. Tiny pinpricks punctured the black velvet of the night sky. There were so many, more than Lorna had ever imagined there could be in the sky. She could not sense herself. She was nobody. Less than a minute speck in the eternal, unending ebb and flow of the universe.

Lorna was nothing. But she was still here, among the exploding, raging, dying and birthing of galaxies, the black holes and magnetospheric eternally collapsing objects.

Suddenly, one star began to burn brighter than the others. Another joined it, then more, until a full constellation had been traced against the inky backdrop of infinity. And somehow, when Lorna looked at it, she could read it just as she read her books and scrolls.

"The darkest days lay yet ahead. With the Reckoning comes an end - yet also a beginning. In the darkest hour, when all has been lost - rebirth. The Legion Queen will come from beyond the Veil, a true daughter of prophecy who will unite the shattered realm. Find her. Guide her. Aid her. The prophecy is in the scroll. The scroll is here, in Castle Bleak, waiting for you, Shadow's sister."

What did it mean? Lorna wanted to ask for answers, but there was no one to beseech, only the cold, unfeeling sky, bright stars dimming one by one around her until just the Void remained... and a voice...

"Are you a halfwit?" Bleakhart rasped.

Lorna's eyes flew open. She found herself lying on the dungeon floor, the stink of filth and excrement pungent in her nostrils, making her gag. A hand clamped down on her shoulder, and she was dragged across the stones, their roughness abrading her face.

"Stop! Stop. Please." She wanted to know more and ask the questions that flitted like a million small, confused birds in her mind, but when she finally forced her eyes open, she found the magical barrier sealed—the elves inside, her outside.

Bleakhart hauled her roughly to her feet. "Never let them touch you. Ever," he growled, glaring at her with his watery eyes, his jowls trembling as he ground his teeth in consternation.

"But–"

He shook her so hard her teeth clamped closed on her tongue, and Lorna tasted the coppery tang of blood in her mouth.

"Don't tell me what you saw, don't tell me what you heard. Not a word about it. And never let them touch you again. Do you understand me?"

Lorna nodded meekly, the pain in her mouth and skull muting her will to protest.

"That's enough for today. Get out. Come back tomorrow, and don't be a bloody fool next time. Never let them touch you."

He emphasized the last words as if they were a mantra, and Lorna wondered what premonition Bleakhart had glimpsed when an elf revealed the strands of his fate to him.

For they had. Lorna could see it in his eyes.

She shook her head to clear it. She would question him on it. But not now. Now, she would follow Bleakhart's finger, pointing out of the dungeon, back the way she had come. Back to fresh air, light, and the safety of her chambers.

Lightheaded, she took careful steps, her feet dragging on the stone, her body feeling weary and spent, her mind a blur.

What did any of it mean? Already the words felt far away, difficult to hold onto. As if they were a dream to slip away upon awakening. *A Reckoning.* She had heard of them, the great gatherings when all the fae lords and ladies of the six courts gathered to make decisions. But there had not been a Reckoning in hundreds of years, not since the early days when the fae were newly arrived in the Ethereal Realms.

And what of the Veil? The Legion Queen? These words were new to her. She'd never come across either before. Were they mysteries of the forgotten past or portents of the future?

She paused, rubbed her temples, and looked around. She had reached a terminus. She could not go straight, nor did she know which of the three paths before her led the way out.

Lorna realized she was lost.

A Trick of the Light

Lorna stared at the stone wall looming before her, blocking the way forward. She twisted her head left then right, peering down the passages on either side of her. Which tunnel led to the surface—the air, Goddess she needed air—and which wound deeper into the abyss, the bowels of the undercity?

Irrational terror seized Lorna, and beads of sweat broke out on her brow as she tried to soothe the panic building in her, threatening to choke off her breath. She tried to convince herself she had no reason to be frightened. She was the empress's sister. Someone would look for her. Osiris. Ereda. Someone. She wouldn't be left down here, forgotten. If she called, Bleakhart would hear her. He would come. But the idea of seeing the wretched sorcerer only kindled a new flame of dark terror inside her, the fear mounting as she stood frozen in indecision.

Lorna sucked down deep breaths of the stale air, chokingly thick with dust and mildew. She wasn't a child, she told herself, and no ghosts wandered the seldom-trod tunnels of the undercity. Only the bones of her ancestors, rotting away, magic long gone from them, no power to hurt her. And the elves, captive in the dungeon—just as powerless.

Still, the idea of being trapped in this vast abandoned network of corridors and chambers made Lorna's heart quicken in her breast and her breathing ragged.

Calm. Calm yourself. You can get out of here.

Lorna closed her eyes and called the shadows. They rushed to her, swirling in her hands. "Show me the way I came," she whispered.

Dim, smoky trails appeared before her, leading down the western pathway—her own magic and Osiris's. Relief washed over her, and the panic squeezing her chest subsided as she followed the trail left behind.

The magical residue led her up, through the cold marble confines of the crypt, and finally to the only way of egress from the necropolis, the towering black door with a golden keyhole. She pulled the key from her bodice and waited for her shaking hands to still before inserting it into the lock. The tumblers clicked, and Lorna shoved the door open, bursting out of the dungeon and into the expansive main hall of Castle Bleak. The diffuse light temporarily blinded her, and she closed her eyes to shield them, swallowing a deep, desperate breath of fresh air.

Lorna opened her eyes, ready to exhale slowly, but her sigh of relief strangled in her throat as she caught sight of Ereda standing inches from the door, watching her. As always, her sister cut an imposing image with the fierce, diamond-patterned snakes writhing in her hair, onyx circlet gleaming on her brow, cloaked in black velvet from head to toe. The form-fitted gown contrasted with her pale gray skin, making her appear the embodiment of the shadows.

"Done so soon?" Ereda arched a black brow, her lips pressed in a tight line of disappointment.

Lorna forced a neutral expression, though she was irritated. Was her sister checking up on her, making sure she was attending to her duties? Surely Osiris had told her he'd delivered her to the undercity.

"Bleakhart said we'd done enough for one day." Lorna broke free from Ereda's judgmental gaze and dropped her eyes, focusing instead on the swirled pattern of the obsidian floor.

"I see." Her sister's tone seemed to imply that she highly doubted that, but it was the truth.

"I had an... incident. With the elves," Lorna confessed, breaking the tense silence between them. She wasn't sure how much she wanted to tell her sister about the elf and her prophecy, but perhaps a few details should appease Ereda. She still felt dazed, as if she was only half in this world and half in another, her mind still floating in a far-off sky where stars raged like bonfires all around her.

"What sort of incident?" Ereda folded her arms across her chest, feigning indifference but leaning forward slightly. Lorna could sense her curiosity was piqued.

Lorna cleared her throat and pulled her gaze up from the floor to meet Ereda's again. "An elf... touched me, and–"

"You're not supposed to let them touch you. Even weakened, they can damage your mind beyond repair if they forge a psychic bond. You, of all people, should know that," the empress snapped.

Lorna nodded meekly. She had known but had done it anyway. Why? Did destiny already have its fingers on her pulse before she even stepped into the dungeon? She couldn't think about it now. Ereda was waiting.

Lorna went on, "I know. I–I wasn't thinking. But she showed me things."

Ereda stroked her chin and studied Lorna, remaining silent but nodding for her to go on.

"She spoke of a prophecy." Lorna could never lie to her sister. Ereda had an uncanny knack for reading people. She knew Lorna's tells, had since she was a child. But surely, a white lie of omission should be safe. She would speak of the prophecy and omit the details about her own link to it.

"Go on." Ereda drummed her nails on her thigh, impatient now.

"It spoke of a Reckoning. Something called 'the Veil' and a unified Ethereal Realms." Seeds sown. Something for Ereda to contemplate and do with what she would.

"A Reckoning," the Shadow Empress mused. "There hasn't been a Reckoning in thousands of years," she dismissed, then paused and tilted her head to the side. "But perhaps... Unity, you said?" Her lips curled up in a slow smile as if puzzle pieces were coming together in her mind. "Yes, a Reckoning."

The distracted expression cleared, and Ereda's eyes grew hard as flint. "I expect you to put in a full day's work down there from now on. I'll speak to Bleakhart to ensure that happens. And don't do anything else stupid like that again. I need you, Lorna."

Ereda turned and walked away, the long train of her gown swishing as it dragged across the floor behind her. Lorna flinched, watching her go. She wanted to believe her sister's words had come from a place of affection, wanted to believe that she cared about her and didn't want the elves to harm her. But deep down, she knew that wasn't the case. Ereda was only interested in herself and her plans.

She watched her sister disappear around the corner and, finally, released a shaky breath.

The afternoon turned to evening. Lorna tried to relax and, when that failed, endeavored to keep herself busy. She had always found peace within her books and scrolls. It was easy to lose herself in the pages, immersed in the rich histories of the Realms and the intricacy of language. But even her books offered no solace tonight. She was antsy, unable to focus. Her attempt at translations made her head ache; not even fantastical myths and legends could hold her interest.

The existence of the elven scroll—and the fact that it

was here, somewhere in Castle Bleak— was like a maggot crawling around in the back of her mind. She tried to crush it, but it kept regenerating, squirming to the forefront of her thoughts like a parasitic worm, gnawing, demanding attention.

She should never have let the elf touch her.

But she had. And now she could feel the sticky web of fate being spun around her.

Lorna stroked the feathers of a quill on her desk, giving in to the temptation of the thoughts. She needed answers. What was written on the scroll, and what was her role in this prophecy? If she found it, would she even be able to translate it? It could be just another indecipherable riddle, like so many of the scrolls she had struggled with.

But if she succeeded...

Not only would her maddening curiosity be sated, but the information might be of value to Ereda. Perhaps the scroll was the key to escaping Bleakhart and his dungeon. She could get back to her books and translations—resume the work she loved.

Lorna slammed the book closed, her mind made up. She would drive herself mad if she stayed cooped up in her tower room brooding about it.

She would try the library. She felt sure she'd looked over every elven scroll on the shelves by this point, so it seemed unlikely that this mysterious prophecy was there...but it couldn't hurt to check again, could it?

Donning her black cloak, she left her chamber and headed down the steep spiral staircase to Castle Bleak's main hall. Her slippered feet whispered over the marble floor as she crossed the expansive space before turning left down a narrow corridor. It was late. The scribes would be gone for the day, but perhaps that was for the best. She could search uninterrupted without them nosing around, haunting her every step.

She reached the library's large, banded iron door, opened it, stepped inside, and smiled. Dust motes hung in the air, glittering in the diffuse glow of lamplight. She breathed deeply. The vanilla and musty biblichor were a restorative to her senses. This was her place, where she felt at home.

Glancing around, Lorna determined she was alone. It was as quiet as the Goddess Xennia's chapel and just as sacred a space to her. She stood motionless, wondering where to begin. Her eyes moved between the rows of tall cherry wood shelves.

Familiar, the same as it has always been, except...

Just a trick of the light, surely, but one shelf seemed to be illuminated. Lorna moved toward it like a moth drawn to an invisible flame. Had she looked at these scrolls before? Lorna wasn't sure. She grazed her fingers over them. Old. Ancient even. Lorna could tell from the quality of the paper and the faded ink. Her heart fluttered in anticipation as she gently unrolled the first one.

Her heart sank.

She couldn't read every word but immediately recognized the names of flowers and herbs. Botany, not prophecy. Disappointed, she rolled the scroll back up and replaced it. She did the same with four more and found herself similarly disappointed. Municipal records of the elven capitals. Rolls of the city residents and their family names. Any other day they might interest her. But right now, they were not what she was looking for.

Lorna was about to give up when her fingers brushed across something peculiar. Perhaps just a knot in the wood? Curious, though. She pressed against the indentation in the back of the shelf. There was a soft click, and what felt like a small panel slid away.

Upon reaching inside, Lorna felt nothing but the smooth hardwood, but then something else. She recognized the texture by touch, not paper, but silken fabric. Lorna willed her hands not to sweat as she ever-so-carefully pulled her discovery from the hidden compartment in the shelf wall.

Before the fae had invaded the Ethereal Realms, when the elven society was at its peak, they had written not on paper but on a kind of parchment made from spider silk. Could it be...?

Lorna examined the missive—It was.

The spider silk scroll was wrapped in a green ribbon and secured with a wax seal she recognized at once as Muírgan Vivane's personal stamp. The elven ruler, reader of the stars, and soothsayer. She had come across her star maps and predictions before.

Lorna hesitated, staring at the scroll that seemed to glow faintly in the wavering lamplight.

The elves claimed one could not evade their destiny. That it was fixed, written in the stars, charted out long before your birth. You might delay it, but the longer you fought against the current of fate, the stronger its pull would become. Until it crashed over you like a tsunami, and when the wave receded, it would sweep you out to sea. They claimed it was better—easier—if you accepted the Goddess's will and swam along with it.

But Lorna wasn't so sure.

She was still staring at the scroll in her trembling hands, deep in thought about what to do with it, when a voice behind her said, "I see you made it out of Bleakhart's lair in one piece."

Lorna startled, her hand flying to her chest, crumpling the scroll against her breast as she wheeled around.

Osiris Bane leaned against a bookshelf near the library entrance. His hair was piled high and tight in a knot at the top of his head, but a few strands had escaped. Instead of his standard black and gray emissary garb with the Shadow crest on the breast, he wore tight, black leather riding pants and a loose gray shirt open at the neck. The lamplight danced across his features, illuminating his strong jaw, the flickering light dancing in his dark eyes.

Lorna's heartbeat picked up, but not for fear of being discovered with the scroll. It was none of Osiris's business what she researched in the library, and it certainly wouldn't cause a stir if he told Ereda she was here. That was nothing out of the ordinary.

No, it wasn't fear, but something else that set her blood pumping hard through her veins. A nameless yearning that she refused to acknowledge. Instead, she looked away, carefully smoothing the scroll in her hands, removing any wrinkles her rough handling might have caused in the ancient fabric.

"You again? How is it that wherever I am, you always seem to be lurking?"

Osiris flashed a quick grin. "I know your haunts, Lorna. Everyone does. You don't exactly keep us on our toes. It stood to reason I'd find you here when you weren't in your chambers. It's a bit late for the blood pools."

Lorna huffed and rolled her eyes. "My sister must be pleased you know my routines so well. I can only assume that your...your...*stalking* is at her behest again? Did she summon me?"

Osiris laughed—a deep gruff sound, but with a warmth that Lorna hated to admit she was fond of. No one else seemed to laugh around Castle Bleak, at least not like Osiris. Sure, the courtiers and servants snickered at her behind her back when they made snide remarks about her bookishness. Even the slaves seemed in on the fun sometimes. But Osiris's chuckle was genuine and not directed at her, as if she were the butt of some rude joke.

"No, Lady Blackburn." Osiris's eyes sparkled with mischief. "But the Empress did send me to deliver some letters today."

She looked up, curious. That explained his disheveled appearance. He must have just returned from hard flying, delivering those missives. And there must have been something extraordinary about the correspondence, or Osiris wouldn't have sought her out in such a state of disarray; he was always so meticulous.

Not that Lorna minded. She found she rather liked seeing him when he wasn't all done up like the court peacock in his fancy, formal get-up.

Keeping her tone as bland as she could muster, Lorna said, "You're an emissary. Your entire purpose in this realm is to deliver messages. So that isn't exactly a surprise."

Lorna thought Osiris would tell her whatever news he had then since he seemed so eager to deliver it. Instead, his lip curled up in a half-smile, and he said, "I hear you had an eventful first day in the dungeons."

Lorna shot him a daggered look. "Yes, I'm sure the whole court knows how stupid Ereda's sister is, letting an elf grab her." She dropped off and waved her free hand dismissively in the air, still clutching the scroll in her other.

Osiris's smile widened, and Lorna could tell he was struggling not to laugh. "No, only me. And those I delivered her letters to today, of course."

Anxiety clenched in Lorna's chest, tightening it and making it hard to breathe. "Her letters... were about me?" She barely managed to get the words out.

Osiris shrugged, then pushed off the bookcase, striding towards her with long steps, his form falling into shadow as he moved. There was something feline about his motions, like a jaguar ready to pounce. His black wings were folded behind him, but plumes of dust from his travel whisked off them, shimmering in the light as he stepped into the lamp's glow beside her.

He was so close she could smell him.

The maddening scent of a nightshade flower that she could never quite place was a constant, but today it mingled with the musk of the forests he'd flown through and a faint smokiness.

Was he in the Court of Flames? Lorna wondered and suppressed a shudder. She had no love for the Lord of

Flames or his hot court full of bubbling magma and fiery-tempered fae.

Osiris leaned toward her and said, in a conspiratorial tone, "Ereda has called a Reckoning. Based on the information you gleaned from the elves."

He paused, then added, almost as an afterthought, "Information you acquired through torture, of course. According to your sister, you're quite accomplished with a whip." Osiris smirked, clearly aware Lorna had little capacity for torture in her.

Alarms sounded in Lorna's head, loud as the bells that chimed in Castle Bleak's high towers when an invading force was at their gates.

Ereda was moving too quickly. Lorna didn't have the slightest idea what the Reckoning she'd seen in her vision had to do with anything. She didn't even know the prophecy or if there really was one. This could have all been a scheme by the elves, a trick to...

The scroll suddenly burned in her hand. She dropped her eyes to it and noticed it glowing faintly. If she wanted answers, this was where she would find them.

"I have to go," Lorna whispered.

She turned away from Osiris, feeling lightheaded; before she could make it to the library doors, her vision was pinpricked with stars. She lurched towards a nearby shelf, leaning against it for support, hunching over to wait for the feeling to pass.

The scroll was still scorching her flesh, but she ignored it, swallowing deep lungfuls of air as she always did when this happened. Just as it had in the tunnel, the panic would pass. It always did.

Osiris was beside her within moments, cupping her chin in his hand and drawing her eyes to meet his. "Are you all right?" His brow furrowed, his expression earnest and full of concern.

Lorna nodded and struggled to find her voice. "I'm fine," she choked out, breaking eye contact.

When she wrenched her face away, Osiris let her go but draped his arm around her for support. Lorna felt the lithe, sinuous muscles through the thin fabric of his shirt, honed from all his flights across the full breadth of the Ethereal Realms delivering Ereda's letters.

She was surprised to find that she didn't want him to let her go, and as he held her, Lorna's breaths became steadier. She felt safe—a foreign sensation.

Osiris gently lifted her to her feet and said, "I'll walk you to your room."

Lorna shook her head. "Osiris, I'm fine."

The scroll still burned.

"I insist. I would be remiss in my duties if I let you walk all that way alone in your current condition." He tossed her a wry smile. "Your sister would have my head if anything were to happen to you."

Lorna couldn't help but chuckle. They both knew that wasn't the case. Ereda would grumble that she'd have to find a new translator, but Lorna doubted she would shed so much as a single tear.

The Slow Burn

Halfway up the narrow spiral staircase leading to her quarters in the tower, Lorna grudgingly admitted to herself that she was glad Osiris had escorted her. Though the panic attack had faded, she still felt woozy and unwell, a dull pain throbbing behind her eyes.

More disconcertingly, the scroll still scorched her palm like a firebrand. It seemed to grow hotter and more demanding every moment she didn't read it. She wanted to drop it, but her fingers remained curled around it like a cursed object she could not escape.

Finally, they reached the top of the stairs, and Osiris opened the door. Just seeing her chamber flooded Lorna with relief.

"You can leave me here. I'll be fine," Lorna told

Osiris, extricating herself from the arm he'd draped over her shoulder and brushing past him.

No one besides herself in all of Castle Bleak had ever been inside Lorna's room before. It was her refuge, her escape. The one place she knew she could always be alone... and just be. No expectations. No demands. No illusions. Just Lorna. Even Ereda granted her this one small boon—a place of her own where she would not be disturbed.

Lorna wasn't sure she wanted that privacy violated.

Osiris shook his head and folded his arms across his chest. "Not going to happen. Not until I'm sure you're all right."

Lorna could tell by his tone that there was no sense in arguing with him, so despite her reservations, she let Osiris take her by the arm and guide her inside. He led her straight to the narrow iron-framed bed, where she sat down and forced a wan smile. Then, with a momentous force of will, Lorna unlocked her fingers from around the scroll and set it down beside her. The ache in her hand dulled but did not go away.

Osiris didn't return her smile. His face was drawn into a concerned expression as he stood above her, arms folded across his chest. What little sunlight the Shadow Court enjoyed had dissipated with the onset of the evening. Lorna couldn't help but notice how the shadows in the room suited Osiris, making him look all the more handsome as they painted over his chiseled features.

Lorna looked away, realizing she was staring at him. "You can go now. I assure you, I'm fine."

Osiris ignored her remark and sat down on the bed beside her. "Lorna, what's going on with you? Did something happen with Bleakhart? Did he make you...do things?"

Lorna shook her head and laughed bitterly. She certainly couldn't blame Bleakhart for this. She'd gotten herself tangled in this web. Her gaze dropped to the scroll on her bed, wondering how much she should tell him.

But before she could voice her concerns, Osiris reached for her. He cupped her cheek in his hand, tilting her face upwards and looking her dead in the eyes.

"I want you to be happy, Lorna," Osiris said.

Happy?

A foreign word for Lorna. She was at peace when she was reading and translating. But happiness? What was it? Beyond getting lost in the fantasies found in a book or the thrill of learning a new symbol? Her entire life had been devoted to her sister's aim of conquest, and she took no joy in the knowledge that with each discovery she made in the elven texts, more beings would fall victim to Ereda's power-hungry crusade.

As far as Lorna knew, she had never been happy. Nor would she ever be. To even hope for something so grandiose as happiness was outside her realm of conception.

She opened her mouth to answer, still unsure what she was going to say, then froze, her words catching in her throat as Osiris leaned in close. His soft lips were so close to hers that they shared the same air, and she could smell the mint and black pepper on his breath.

Lorna's heart stuttered, and a tiny gasp escaped her

the moment before Osiris kissed her. The gentle pressure of flesh on flesh took her by surprise. Was it always so tender? Did it always make things stir in one's belly, like shadow moths flitting around? She didn't know. She had never been kissed before.

When Osiris's tongue darted out to moisten her lips and gently probed her mouth, Lorna trembled inside; the fluttering wings of desire beat against her rib cage, desperate to be released. She had dreamt of this kiss in lonely, private moments when she wished things could be different but never dared believe that it could happen.

As Osiris pulled away, Lorna tried to pretend she didn't feel the deep, almost soul-crushing emptiness that returned as the yearning inside her stilled once more.

She could not allow it to happen.

"What the hell was that?" Lorna barely got the words out between ragged breaths.

Osiris blinked, then his eyes widened, and Lorna had never seen him look so disarmed. Gone was the cool calculation, the mocking joviality. He looked like she felt... stunned, bewildered, and desperate with unsated desire.

Lorna's lower lip trembled, her eyes brimming with barely contained tears as the longing for something that could never be threatened to choke her.

When Osiris noticed her expression had changed, he stuttered, "I'm sorry. I don't know—I didn't mean to... it's just that–" He grabbed Lorna's left hand, the one that had held the scroll. It stung, but she barely noticed. "Lorna, I've wanted to do that for a century at least."

A century? Lorna's mind reeled, and panic flared.

She'd known it, yes. But no. They could not do it. There were a thousand reasons why. Osiris was arrogant and condescending, and when they were young, he used to pull her hair and conjure up shadow beasts to chase her around and frighten her. He was a courier, an errand boy, with no real standing in the court—a climber, as Ereda said.

And she was the Shadow empress's sister. She could do nothing without Ereda's blessing.

But it was so hard to deny him when he sat so close that she could feel his warmth, and so beautiful, with stray dark curls framing his face and his steel gray eyes shimmering. And he could be kind, which was more than Lorna could say for anyone else in the Court of Shadows. He tried to take care of her and made her smile and...

No. It can not be. Stop it now before it goes too far.

Lorna vaulted to her feet and pointed to the door. "Get out."

At first, Osiris just looked confused. Then his expression crumpled to that of a wounded child. A pang of regret stabbed through Lorna's heart, and her hand trembled and burned anew, but she didn't lower it.

She had enough problems without adding a love affair with Osiris Bane to the mix.

"Lorna, I'm sorry. I didn't mean to take liberties, but if you only knew..."

Lorna's wings extended to their full span behind her, and the shadows curled in from the corners of the room.

"Osiris, get out," she commanded, magic brewing in a dark, silent storm around her.

Osiris winced, then rose as if his body were a thousand-pound weight, dragging himself toward the door as if every step was an agony. When he reached it, he turned around and said over his shoulder, "I've always loved you, Lorna Blackburn. And I know you know it. I don't know if you're blind, scared, or a fool, but this could be the best thing that's ever happened to either of us."

Then he walked out, closing the door behind him with a soft click.

Lorna dropped back onto the bed, shaken.

Her eyes fell to the scroll.

With Osiris's exit, the fight in her dissipated. The shadows that had collected around her dispersed, and she folded her wings. Her lips still tingled from the unexpected kiss, and her heart pounded in a too-fast, staccato rhythm, not pleasant like the moths in her belly but like a creature trapped and struggling to break free.

Osiris was a fool if he thought there could ever be anything between them. And she was just as much a fool for being so...drawn to him. She should never have let him in her room nor let him presume it was all right to get close to her. But most of all, she should never have given in to those feelings she'd denied for so long.

It could only end in heartbreak for them both.

Her head still ached dully, and her thoughts ran wild, out-of-control paths through her mind. She was confused and drained. It felt like her whole life had been altered in the course of a single day. She longed to plunge into the solace of slumber and was about to curl up in her bed and give in to her exhaustion.

But the scroll held her gaze. She couldn't ignore the pull of it. Tendrils of magic curled off it, beckoning her, glittering gold in the dim light of her chamber.

Lorna couldn't resist the urge to read it.

She picked up the parchment and slipped a fingernail beneath the wax seal to pull it away, careful to keep the insignia intact. Muírgan's seal was a rare and valuable thing. The elven queen was thousands of years old, one of the oldest elves who remained free in the Realms. She had begged asylum in the Court of Dreams, and the Dreamers had granted it. Much to Ereda's chagrin, for from there, Muírgan and her people launched counter-strikes against the Courts of Shadow and Flame.

Strange, then, that one of her scrolls was hidden in the false wall on a shelf in the library of the Court of Shadows. Who put it there?

A question, Lorna realized, she would likely never know the answer to.

With trembling hands, she unrolled the silken fabric, then gazed at the swirling golden symbols decorating the page. While she hadn't expected to be able to read all of them, she should be able to make out at least a few.

But Lorna couldn't decipher the glyphs.

Not a single one.

She strained her eyes, focusing on the swirling runes. Row after row of them streamed across the page in an elaborate scrawl, but none were familiar.

"That doesn't make sense," Lorna whispered,

furrowing her brow and biting her lip. She rubbed her eyes and tried again.

Still, the meaning of the runes eluded her.

The old tongue, she realized. Muírgan must have scribed them before the fae and mortals had bastardized the elven language.

Lorna's contemplation was suddenly interrupted by a shooting pain in her hand. She dropped the scroll with a sharp hiss and raised her shaking palm to examine it, bringing her other hand to her mouth and smothering the scream that threatened to emerge from her throat. Etched into her flesh was a glowing symbol. It resembled a tree, with winding limbs and roots connected to form a circle.

Her mind raced. How had it gotten there? Was it the elf's doing or the scroll's? What did it mean, and why did it look so familiar? Lorna had seen it before; she was sure of it. But where? She racked her brain. The answer danced just beyond her reach, taunting her.

She rubbed her temples. The ache from the blow to her head had returned, now coupled with a tension headache brought on by her frustration over Osiris Bane's unexpected amorous overture.

Perhaps that was it. Lorna was simply overwrought. She glanced at her hand again, half expecting that the glyph emblazoned there would be gone, nothing more than a hallucination.

But the mark remained, flickering from red to gold against her dark skin.

Blood Magic

L orna was basking in the hazy glow of half-sleep when the knock sounded. She did not recall falling asleep, but she apparently had at some point. Still fully clothed, her robes were rumpled from tossing and turning. She brushed the sleep-mussed tangles of her hair, which she generally braided before bed, from her eyes.

The knock sounded again.

Lorna sat up, wincing as the pain in her head and hand brought the previous day's calamities rushing back to her. The elf's vision. The prophecy. The scroll. And, oh Goddess, Osiris Bane.

Spasms of dread crept into Lorna's heart as she held her right hand up to examine it. The brand was still there, though it had faded some; not a trick of her imagination after all.

Lorna groaned, wishing she could dive underneath the covers and fall back into the blissful ignorance of sleep, but the knocking grew more insistent. Before she could get both feet on the cold marble floor, the door flew open with a crash and a squeal of the hinges.

Ereda stood in the doorway. Lorna's first impulse was irritation. That was twice in as many days the sanctity of her chambers had been violated. Could she not even have this one place? This one safe space to call her own?

But as the last cobwebs cleared from her mind, Lorna registered the bright light streaming through her window. It had to be half past mid-sun! She tensed, her body going rigid as aggravation shifted to alarm and anticipation of the tongue-lashing she was about to receive from her sister.

"You're late to meet with Bleakhart. That's not like you. And Osiris says you were unwell last night. So, what's the matter with you?" Ereda tilted her head to the side, studying her sister.

Of course, Osiris had run to Ereda about the episode in the library. He was her emissary, and it was his duty, which was precisely why Lorna could not trust him. Any guilt she'd felt at rejecting him vanished with this small treason exposed. She should have known to expect it.

Lorna squeezed her hand into a fist, lowered it to her side, hiding the mark, then slid off the bed.

Dipping into a low, respectful bow, she said, "I'm sorry, Your Majesty. Yesterday was a difficult day–"

Ereda's impatient growl silenced Lorna's attempt at an apology.

"You are weak." The Shadow empress pounded her

fist into her hand, and long, curling tendrils of shadow steamed off it. "It's time you grew out of your sullen, childish, dramatic ways. Lorna, you are my sister. I need you strong and ready to fight by my side."

Lorna bowed her head, studying the whorled patterns on the floor. How quickly things changed. Yesterday Ereda had been lauding her as a hero in missives to all the courts. Now, she was on the Shadow Empress's blacklist once again.

She longed to tell her sister that she could not change what she was—who she was—just to appease her. But the argument would get her nowhere. It would only stoke the embers of Ereda's wrath into a raging fire. Instead, Lorna replied, "You are right, sister. I will try harder."

As the shadows elongated and spread through the room, distinct notes of resin and camphor, the scent of Ereda's magic, filled the air, burning Lorna's throat. The darkness was drawn to Ereda, blackening her skin as it moved over her in amorphous patterns like a diaphanous, ever-shifting veil.

"I don't want you to try. I need you to do," the Shadow Empress hissed. She heaved a sigh. "I've called a Reckoning."

Lorna knew this but did not let on that she did. She forced a neutral expression, waiting for her sister to go on, but Ereda only stared at her, her face unreadable. An uncomfortable silence stretched between them until Lorna finally asked, "For what purpose?"

"To solidify an alliance. You will join me there. But for now"—Ereda appraised Lorna, her gaze raking her from head to toe—"make yourself presentable and go see Bleakhart in the undercity. He has a special project for you."

Lorna could conceive of nothing she was less inclined to do than revisit the dungeons. And no one she was less eager to see than Bleakhart. The very thought of it flipped her stomach and made her nauseous.

Grasping at straws, she reached for the scroll on the bed, then held it out toward Ereda. "Sister, I've found something."

Lorna held her breath as the Shadow empress's gaze flicked to the scroll. Interest kindled in Ereda's violet eyes, but it was fleeting.

"What does it say?" Ereda inquired.

Lorna cleared her throat. "I'm not sure yet, but—"

The Shadow empress scoffed. "Then it's of no use to me now. Go seek Bleakhart. You can dicker with your books and scrolls on your own time. This is more important."

Osiris was absent from the door to the undercity when Lorna approached. As much as she had wanted him gone after the ill-advised kiss, she secretly wished he was waiting for her now, with a smile and a kind word. But there was no sign of him, not even a trace of his scent, a faint glimmer of his magic.

She lingered for a few moments, hoping he would round the corner and offer to escort her, but when he did not, she pulled the key from her pocket and slipped it into the lock. The door, solid metal and heavy, opened with a pained creak that set Lorna's nerves on edge and made her grind her teeth.

Subconsciously, the fingers of her right hand to her other palm. The rune pulsed with warmth, and there was something oddly comforting about the sensation.

Lorna walked, following the narrow tunnel that led through the crypt without so much as a glance at the sarcophagus this time. The cold marble effigy of her mother could offer her no comfort, and whatever wisdom her ancestors held was forever lost to the Void with their magic.

Besides, she didn't have time to linger. Ereda had made her urgency clear, and she'd already wasted time waiting for Osiris.

She had no trouble finding her way down to Bleakhart's lair this time. Like muscle memory, her eyes adjusted to the darkness at once when she reached the lower levels. She found the door to his study closed and raised her hand to knock, but before she could rap on it, Bleakhart's voice sounded behind her.

"I'm glad you made it. We have a great deal of work to do today. I trust you learned your lesson after last week. Although, this is a different sort of work entirely."

What does he mean by that? Lorna turned around to face Bleakhart, eyeing him warily. His expression was as dour as ever, but she got the impression he was nervous about something. He was hunched over, the curvature of his spine more pronounced than usual, his skeletal frame rigid, black wings with erratic clumps of red feathers pulled in tight at his shoulders.

Lorna fidgeted, knotting the fabric of her robes

between her fingers, waiting for him to go on. When he didn't, and the silence stretching between them grew too awkward for her to stand, she said, "My sister said it was very important. But she did not give me any details. What will we be doing?"

Bleakhart inhaled a rasping breath, then jerked around, pivoting on his heel. "Come with me," he said without further explanation as he shuffled down the hall in the opposite direction of the way they had gone the previous day.

Lorna followed him. The walls narrowed around her, and the claustrophobic sensation tightened her chest. Every muscle in her body protested, but she put one foot in front of the other. Screams faded in and out, but the acoustics of the underground tunnels made it impossible to tell if they were moving toward or away from the sounds. Still, the pained cries made the hairs on the back of Lorna's neck stand up, and goosebumps prickled her skin.

Finally, Bleakhart stopped in front of a narrow, windowless door. It was unlike the rest of the doors she had seen in the dungeon, which were barred, exposing the occupants, and something sinister about it made Lorna's skin crawl. Faint arcane energy, blue with black flecks, swirled around the door. Not Shadow magic or Fire. Something darker. Older. Magic with a sharp, acrid bite to the scent.

It's just a door, she told herself, swallowing a gag as the magic's scent wafted into her nostrils. *Who knows what's behind it? It might not be anything menacing at all. It could be a room full of books,* she reasoned.

But when Bleakhart turned his head and looked at her, his grin told her that whatever it was, Lorna would not like it.

"Are you ready?" he asked.

Was she? Of course not. How could she prepare herself for the unknown? Lorna wanted to turn and run back to the surface, far from the undercity. She wanted to find Osiris and have him wrap her in his arms, enveloping her in the safety of his embrace. She wanted to beg him to take her away from her sister, from Bleakhart, from the undercity. They could flee to the Court of Dreams, seek asylum there, and be together, far from the horrors of slavery, torture, and Ereda's war.

But she knew Osiris would never do that. No matter how much he claimed he loved her, he loved the climb more. He craved the rush from each rung as he ascended the ladder toward nobility. He was driven to make a name for himself. Nor would Lorna shirk her responsibilities to her sister and her people, truth be told. They were her birthright, and she could not forsake them.

So as loath as she was to find out what fresh horrors of Ereda and Bleakhart's design were hidden behind the door, Lorna whispered, "I'm ready."

She expected Bleakhart to open the door using a spell. That was the only magic she knew: words of power uttered to bend a fae's bloodline element under the spellcaster's control. Instead, he reached into the pocket of his black robes adorned with the Shadow Court crest and pulled out a serrated-edged black athame with a tapered, needle-point tip.

Lorna's breath hitched. Before she could regain her

voice to protest, Bleakhart had slashed the blade across his wrinkled, papery-skinned palm. Blood beaded in a thin purplish line—an unusual color, the result of his mixed bloodline, Lorna assumed.

She wasn't particularly squeamish about blood in general—one couldn't be when dwelling in the Shadow Court. The rivers ran with it, down from the jagged mountain peaks that formed a protective wall around Castle Bleak, and no ceremony was complete without a plethora of rituals requiring blood-letting as a cleanse.

But to see it used in magic sent a chill through her that started at her toes and followed her spine up to the nape of her neck.

This was not the Goddess's power but the forbidden magic of dark, primordial gods, long ago outlawed and supposedly forgotten, buried by the elves, never to be uncovered.

But here, deep in the bowels of the earth, it had been rekindled. And Lorna wondered, was anything powerful ever truly forgotten? Or was it just put aside for a time? Lost only until someone somewhere had a need for it again?

Lorna's rune sent another rush through her, hot this time—like a warning.

She watched as Bleakhart pressed his bloodied hand to the door. Flecks of blue and black magic skittered across its surface like tiny ants scuttling to their hill, amassing in a whirling circle around the old sorcerer's hand. The glinting particles spun like a tempest for a moment, then seemed to coalesce into his skin, streaking across his fingers up to his wrist like a spiderweb of blue and black bruises.

Bleakhart's face contorted into a grimace as he wrenched his hand away and took a step back. All color had drained from his skin, and he looked gray and haggard, as if he'd aged centuries during the brief moment of contact with the dark magic.

But his actions had not been in vain. The door began to open slowly, emitting a low, mournful howl as it scraped across the stone floor.

Lorna brought her hands to her ears to block out the anguished sound. It was as if the most lost, hopeless soul was releasing its misery upon the world as, inch by inch, the door slid away to reveal a space kept hidden by such an ancient and terrible boundary.

She didn't want to look but couldn't pull her eyes away.

The interior was more of a cramped pit than a room or a cell. Steps led down into a chamber with a large stone slab in its center, not unlike the one the Shadow empress slept upon to harden herself to pain and discomfort. On it lay the prone form of a woman. An elf, as Lorna could see from the sharply curved ears peeking out from the tangled rat's nest of silver hair that obscured her face.

Clad in tattered rags that had most certainly been fine Elven silk once long ago, she was shackled at the wrists and ankles, with heavy chains securing her to the table.

Bleakhart, seeming to regain his wherewithal after the ordeal with the blood magic, stepped through the now-open door. Lorna was again struck by the urge to run. Whatever she would be asked to do here in this chamber cursed by dark, abandoned gods, she knew it would be terrible.

But she was also drawn to follow. Who was this elf, and why was she here, not in the cells with the others? There was something odd about her bearing, but from this distance, Lorna couldn't figure out what.

She stepped inside.

Her slippers scuffed on the rough stone steps as she crept down them behind Bleakhart. The bitter tang of blood magic intensified, and she pressed the sleeve of her robes to her face to try to dull it.

When she reached the bottom of the pit, she gazed at the elf from a short distance away. Lacerations covered her torso, and her legs were bent at odd, impossible angles.

It was then Lorna realized what had struck her as off.

The elf was dead. No rise and fall of her chest to indicate breath, no sign of magic—the spark that kept all immortal beings alive in the Ethereal Realms.

But why chain a dead elf? Surely she had been no threat to Bleakhart in her current condition, with two broken legs and wounds of this nature.

Lorna looked away, turning from the grotesque scene to Bleakhart. Had Ereda forced her down here just to torture her? To expose her to all the horrors she'd worked so hard to pretend were not happening every day beneath her very feet?

"Why have you brought me here?" she snapped, meeting Bleakhart's stoic, emotionless gaze.

The sorcerer cocked his head and rubbed his jaw, streaking it with purple blood from the wound in his hand.

"To show you," he said simply.

Lorna narrowed her eyes. "Show me what? A dead elf?"

Bleakhart's gaze shifted to the elf, and a shadow of a smile crossed his lips.

"She is dead, isn't she?"

Lorna didn't respond. She just kept her gaze locked on his watery eyes, waiting for an answer.

Bleakhart reached into his pocket and pulled out a crystal vial. Inside, a viscous fluid swirled, black and blue like the magic coating the door. He held the vial up and tapped it with his thumb.

"But not for long."

Defiance

Lorna stood frozen, paralyzed with uncertainty, as Bleakhart approached the broken body on the table with the mysterious tincture in hand. She knew this was wrong and wanted to shout for him to stop, to reach out and pull him back. To put an end to whatever this madness was.

But she didn't.

She couldn't.

Whatever this foul, magical experiment was, it was important to Ereda. If Lorna sabotaged it, her sister's wrath would hang over her like a guillotine blade ready to fall. She was already a disappointment. Had already failed her sister too many times.

So she watched, pensive, as Bleakhart kneeled beside the body and pulled the athame from his belt again.

He grabbed the elf's hand and flipped her arm so the

71

silver-blue veins of her inner forearm were visible. The slave couldn't have been dead long because the limbs were still pliable, there was no rigor mortis, and the veins hadn't yet gone black and collapsed.

Lorna winced, a shudder seizing her as Bleakhart drew the blade's sharp edge along the delicate skin, slicing the elf's arm from elbow to wrist.

"What are you doing?" she croaked.

"Unveiling our new weapon." Bleakhart didn't look up from his work, peeling the skin and flesh aside until the ivory bone showed through.

When he was finished and the limb flayed open, he set the arm back on the table. The semi-coagulated blood ran in thick, slow-moving rivers, dripping from the elf's fingertip and hitting the floor like a slow, terrible rain.

Then he raised the vial and pulled the stopper free. The aroma of the magic was sweet but rancid, like fruit left to rot on the vine in the heat of summer.

Bleakhart leaned over and was about to pour the concoction into the open wound, but he paused as Lorna cried, "No, no, you can't. It's against every law—"

The sorcerer's head snapped up.

"What laws?" he growled. "The ones the elves devised and ascribe to with such unwavering, fanatical tenacity that, for all their power, they're too weak to protect themselves, leaving their entire race on the brink of extinction?" He paused, his lips twisting into a sneer. "Or maybe you mean the laws of the Fae courts, which forbid me to marry or breed because of the mixed blood in my veins. The laws that made it so that my only option for survival was to accept a position down here doing this when I was just a whelp like you?"

He swept his arm in a gesture encompassing not just the elf but also the room and the undercity as a whole, then resumed. "I don't heed your laws. I don't follow your rules. I do what the empress tells me, so I keep my head on my shoulders. I'm not ready to disappear into the Void yet. And I advise you to do the same. You're different, not like the others in the Shadow Court. And it doesn't matter if Blackburn blood runs in your veins or if the empress is your sister. You're just like me, and they'll tear you down and throw you to the wolves the same as they would do to me if they could, *Lorna Blackburn*."

He spat her name like it was a slur, and Lorna sucked in a sharp breath as the words hit home. "You're wrong. I'm nothing like you," she whispered, fighting back the stinging tears threatening to spring from her eyes.

But in her heart, she knew Bleakhart was right. She was only tolerated in the Shadow Court because she was useful and no one dared defy her sister. A second daughter had no purpose but to serve. And because of that, Lorna would do nothing to stop him, even though everything inside her screamed that she must.

With Lorna standing by tight-lipped and silent, Bleakhart resumed his work. He spilled the serum into the wound, the substance hissing and bubbling as it made contact with flesh, blood, and bone. Then he stepped back, folded his arms across his chest, and waited.

"What will happen?" Lorna murmured, watching as

the potion leaked into the cadaver, turning the skin black as it spread.

Bleakhart tilted his hand from side to side. "Ideally? Reincarnation. The perfect warrior. Cheap. Disposable. Its only drive being to kill and gorge herself on flesh." He paused, studying Lorna. "But I haven't perfected it. That's why I need you. To help me figure out what I've got wrong."

Lorna wrapped her arms around herself protectively, and the warmth of her rune pulsed into her, hot and angry like a burning ember. Telling her this was wrong and she could not allow it to stand.

She ignored its warning.

"What's wrong with them?" It made her sick to ask. She wanted no part of this. But if it would get her back in Ereda's good graces once and for all... if it could get her out of this hell hole...

Bleakhart pressed a finger to his lips and pointed at the corpse. "Just watch," he said.

Lorna didn't want to watch, but she couldn't tear her eyes away.

Thankfully, she didn't have to wait long.

It began with the extremities. The corpse's toes twitched, then its fingers curled in, gripping the table so hard its fingernails splintered.

Then the elf's back spasmed, arching away from the stone, before falling again with a dull thud. The broken legs kicked, despite the savage wounds, bone fragments clearly visible through the compound fractures.

It actually works, she thought, morbid fascination warring with abject terror and disgust in her mind.

This was necromancy—wretched, forbidden—and the implications were far-reaching. If the Shadow empress had the power to reanimate those who fell in battle—whatever side the combatants were on—it could quickly turn the tide of the war with the elves. It wasn't lost on Lorna that, if what Bleakhart said was true, casualties would no longer be a liability. It would be impossible for them to lose.

No wonder Ereda was so insistent that she needed to help Bleakhart.

Suddenly there was stillness again. The body stopped seizing and flopped back onto the table, a limp, boneless thing. Its head was twisted to the side, and eyes clouded with blue and black whorls stared unblinking at Lorna.

She shuddered as the rune sent a pulse of heat straight to her heart.

Nevertheless, Lorna turned to Bleakhart and asked, "Now what?" her voice a strangled whisper.

Bleakhart clenched his teeth, his jaw muscle ticking. He stared at the body as if willing something more from it. But nothing happened. It just lay there in a state of suspended animation. "Now, nothing," he answered, sounding piqued. "That is the problem. I have worked the spell this far. I can create a spark of magic to give them new life. Unlife, so to speak, for if you put your finger here"—the sorcerer reached for the arm he had not slashed and pressed his fingers to the sickly blue-grey skin—"There is no pulse. No lifeblood flowing through the veins. Only the faintest current of magic. Not alive, but not dead either. An in-between of sorts."

A dim flicker of hope flashed in Lorna's mind.

Perhaps this was it then—as far as the blood magic could go. They could temporarily recreate the most primitive semblance of life, but it could do no more.

But Bleakhart went on. "We know it is possible to resurrect sentients. Not as they were, but of a sort. Creatures that can walk and talk. Creatures that hunger. Creatures that kill and—"

Lorna didn't want to think about that, so she cut him off before he could continue touting the capabilities of the monsters he hoped to create. "How do you know it's possible?"

"Because they told me so."

She didn't have to ask who 'they' were. It was clear he was referring to the elves. But that didn't mean it was true. This could be a well-planned diversion. Or perhaps the elven prisoners were just telling Bleakhart what he wanted to hear.

"Isn't it possible they lied? Torture a person enough, and they're liable to tell you just about anything," Lorna pointed out.

Bleakhart sneered. "You wound me, Lorna Blackburn." His voice was thick with contempt again. "Do you think implements of suffering are the only tools of my trade? Do I look like one of those brutes your sister keeps by her side who wields cruelty like a sword? Without a care? Have you never heard the saying you catch more bats with shadow wine—"

"—than with vinegar," she finished for him.

Of course, she knew the expression. She just didn't realize Bleakhart had the finesse to kill them with kindness rather than the whip.

"So you bribed them."

Bleakhart nodded, and his sneer twisted into something more cunning and sinister. "But you, my dear, are far sweeter than I could ever aspire to be. And you know their language. It shouldn't be hard for you to figure out what we've got wrong."

And with that, Lorna knew what the sorcerer wanted her to do. Take on his role of confessor. Lull the captive elves into a false sense of safety. And unearth the secrets he could not. Secrets that she was quite sure were better left buried.

"I trust I'll have your assistance in this?" Bleakhart's tone broached no argument as he gave Lorna a steady, penetrating look, red flames dancing in his dark eyes.

Lorna didn't answer immediately. She studied the catatonic elf lying on the stone pyre; her broken body twisted even more unnaturally following the spasms, clouded eyes staring sightlessly into the distance, focused on nothing. The rune burned hotter than any torch on Lorna's hand, and the pain took her breath away for a moment.

When she finally spoke, she uttered a single word.

"No."

It seemed to surprise even Lorna when the word fell from her lips. As her voice echoed the syllable off the stone walls, she brought her hand up to cover her mouth as if she could take it back, return it from whence it came.

But she could not. Once spoken, it could not be undone.

Bleakhart glared at her, his eyes simmering like two

hot coals as his haggard, mismatched wings flared out behind him.

"What did you say?"

Again, Lorna hesitated. Every fiber of her being that valued her life screamed for her to agree to Bleakhart's demands. But some other part of her, long suffocated beneath the binds of self-preservation, broken by years of bowing to every command, broke free and bucked against the sorcerer's order.

Sparks of blue flame cloaked in tendrils of shadow danced at Bleakhart's fingertips, but Lorna knew he would not harm her. Not without Ereda's blessing.

"No. I won't do it."

"I will ask you once more, and I suggest you reconsider your answer. Because to defy me in this is to defy your sister, Empress Ereda Blackburn."

He stared at her hard, and when he spoke again, he did so very slowly, enunciating each word like Lorna was a child or a simpleton who had not understood the question. "I'm not asking you to beat them or kill them. Just to get the answers out of them with that silver tongue and those sweet words of yours. Now, will you do it?"

Every muscle in Lorna's body felt coiled like a spring ready to snap. She trembled from head to toe but forced her chin up so her eyes met Bleakhart's glare when she said, "There are some things Ereda cannot force me to do. Things she cannot know, power she cannot wield. For the good of the Ethereal Realms, my answer is no. This is blood magic, death magic. It was banned for a reason. You may think you can control it —my sister may think she can—but it is wild, the untamed power of dead Gods. In the end, it will destroy you and—"

Bleakhart cut her off with a sibilant hiss. "Silence, you ignorant child."

He didn't shout. His voice was barely more than a whisper, but the disgust it contained was terrifying.

He lunged for Lorna and took her by the arm.

She gasped and tried to pull free of the half-fire fae, but his grip was firm, his sharp-nailed fingers digging into her flesh.

"How dare you lay hands on me? I am a Blackburn. Daughter of one empress, sister to another," Lorna seethed.

"You are nothing but a fool," Bleakhart thundered.

Then his voice dropped again to a low, urgent whisper. "You would sacrifice your future, perhaps even your life, for this?" He turned his head and spat, a globule of spittle landing on the unfortunate elf's forehead. The poor creature twitched slightly but did not blink or move to wipe the droplet away.

"You would betray your ruler, all your people, for what? To protect a dying race that will not even use their own power to defend themselves?"

Though she could not say why, all fear left Lorna at that moment. Whether it was the hand of fate guiding her, the strange rune filling her with bravery, or her mind finally reaching a breaking point, she could not turn back now.

Her trembling stopped, and she shook her head, looking Bleakhart dead in the eye as shadows swirled in from the corners of the room, flitting across her form.

"I don't refuse you for the Elves. Or not for them alone. But for everyone. Because this is bigger than you or me or my sister and her endless war machinations. The destruction Ereda could reap, the repercussions if mistakes were made. Do you not see that this is necromancy? The blackest of evils?"

Bleakhart only sighed. Suddenly, he looked bent and decrepit as he folded his wings and crumpled back into his usual hunched stature. His grip on Lorna's arm loosened, but he did not let go.

"Very well, then," he said, sounding weary. "Let us go see your sister."

A muscle in his cheek twitched, and for a moment, he looked like he was about to say more. But he only clenched his jaw, looked away and began to walk, hauling Lorna along with him through the darkened corridors of the undercity.

Whatever strange fire had filled Lorna dissolved as ice-cold fear sluiced through her veins.

She had defied her sister, the Shadow Empress's, command.

And she feared the cost would be more than she could bear.

Threads of Destiny

Walking briskly, Bleakhart dragged Lorna through the winding tunnels, up past the crypt, where she was sure the eyes of her mother's statue regarded her with dismay, and finally, to the castle proper.

Ordinarily, she would have been relieved as the fresh air purged the subterranean stink from her nose. But she knew where they were going. Even the dungeons deep in the bowels of Castle Bleak seemed less daunting than Ereda's throne room, where she would have to stand before the empress and explain herself.

Why had she refused Bleakhart? What had she been thinking? It wasn't in her nature to do something like that.

The rune etched into her palm throbbed, but she noticed it no more than she did the fact that her whole body was shaking. Panic in her mind dulled all physical sensations.

Bleakhart didn't slow his pace as they passed through the great hall, then paused at the terminus before two massive casement doors leading to the throne room. The sorcerer nodded to the two guards clad in gleaming black plate armor on either side of the entry. They didn't bow; Bleakhart was not royalty to them, favored by Ereda or not, but they stepped forward and flung wide the doors, announcing, "Sorcerer Bleakhart and the Shadow empress's sister, Lorna Blackburn."

At the last second, before passing through those doors to a doom she could not even begin to envision, Lorna tried to wrench free. But she could not break free from Bleakhart's vice-like grip on her wrist. And so he hauled her in with him, her fear a weight that bowed her head and slumped her shoulders.

The doors slammed closed behind them, leaving no hope of escape. A few strategically cast sconces cast pools of light around the massive space, cloaking the rest of the room in the deep, black velvet of shadows.

With her gaze down, Lorna could only see the polished marble steps and the foot of the onyx throne, a flash of Ereda's black lace gown.

"What is the meaning of this?"

Lorna's eyes were forced up as the cold monotone of her sister's voice cut through the chamber. Ereda looked every inch an empress, glaring down at Lorna with the black zirconium circlet set low on her brow and the snakes in her hair writhing and twisting. Her arms were folded across her chest, and her violet eyes blazed, shifting from Lorna to Bleakhart.

"My most esteemed empress"—Lorna had to fight not to roll her eyes—"I regret to inform you that your sister, who should be your strongest ally and do all that is in her power to aid you, refused the task which I set her to. The one you selected her personally for."

The guards at the doors were clearly not privy to Ereda's machinations with the Elves and the blood magic, so Bleakhart kept his words vague.

Ereda's scowl became more pronounced, and the snakes more active, snapping their fanged mouths, forked tongues tasting the air, expressing their empress's displeasure.

"Sister, is this true?"

Lorna dropped to her knees. She had made up her mind on her way up from the catacombs. She would beg for her sister's forgiveness; agree to do whatever she asked of her going forward. What else could she do? She could not be in open defiance of Ereda's commands, no matter how grotesque and dangerous. It was a moment of madness that had struck her; that was all.

"Sister," Lorna began, still on her knees, "you know I have always had the weakness of a gentle heart and have been plagued by an unfortunate loathing for violence."

Ereda bared her teeth and growled low in her throat, an animalistic sound that commanded Lorna to submit. And Lorna trembled at the sound, lowering herself so that her head was almost pressed to the floor.

"I do not need you to remind me how pathetic you are. Is this your excuse, then? That your... bizarre sensitivities made it impossible to follow Bleakhart's command, which was, rest assured, a direct order from me, your empress?"

Lorna wanted to say yes. She had planned to apologize and accept whatever monstrous punishment Ereda devised for her shortcomings. But now, in the moment, Lorna felt that same sensation she'd succumbed to when she defied Bleakhart. It welled up in her...the burning need to defend her actions, to refuse to admit she was in the wrong.

And so she rose.

Setting her jaw, she locked eyes with the Shadow empress and, in a voice that somehow did not shake, said:

"What you are doing is against the laws of the Fae, the Elves, even Humankind. I will play no role in it."

The Shadow empress rasped out a deep, throaty laugh as if the words Lorna had spoken were the most amusing thing she had heard in all her long days. The laughter echoed in the massive stone chamber, then just as abruptly, faded into a quiet so pervasive that every breath Lorna took seemed to hang in the air, testaments to her fear.

The sneer on Ereda's face shifted, her expression becoming as blank and unreadable as the carved stone statues that towered on either side of the massive onyx throne upon which the empress was perched.

Ereda rose with a swish of black satin, took a step toward her sister, and said, "So, it's true. You dare defy me. I always knew you had a traitor's heart."

Lorna wanted to protest, to explain that since they had been children, she had done nothing but obey and try her hardest to please her sister. But before she could force out even a word to defend herself, there was a great crack, like crystals shattering. All light was swallowed up as the torches were snuffed with a splutter and a hiss.

Shadows slithered from the far corners to pool at Ereda's feet, taking the forms of dark vestiges with snapping teeth and sharp claws encircling the empress. Shadows manifested as monsters with black, empty eyes and long twisted limbs.

Lorna tried to tell herself the shadow fiends wouldn't hurt her, for she, too, was of the shadows, but she couldn't make herself believe it. Would these creatures not do the bidding of their leader over all others? The ravenous gleam of their coal-black eyes told Lorna that, given the command, they would obey Ereda. Though the same blood ran through their veins, these were the empress's creatures, not Lorna's. They felt no love or care for her, only the desire to do as they were bid.

Lorna shrank back as the conjured nightmares drifted down the steep stairs of the dais and slunk toward her. The cold sweat of fear beaded on her brow and soaked her pits as the shadow fiends crossed the throne room, getting closer, inch by inch.

She considered conjuring a shadow fiend of her own, but what use would that be? Ereda's beasts would tear it limb from limb; such was her power. And then Lorna would have a second treason to account for. She wanted to scream and plead for her life. To remind Ereda that they were blood and had once shared a womb. But only the words, "Please, sister," made it out past her lips in a strangled whimper.

Ereda did not react to her plea. She stood motionless and grim, not relishing Lorna's suffering as she did the agony of so many, but not calling off the demons that stalked toward her.

All hope is lost. This will be my end, Lorna realized. She would die by her sister's hand, in the palace's throne room where she had been born, for the simple transgression of refusing to do the unthinkable at Ereda's command.

Lorna tried to resign herself to this inevitability. Hadn't she always known that one day it would come to this? She had never had it in her to be what her sister–what everyone–expected her to be.

But something else called to her. The strange compulsion Lorna had felt before when in possession of the scroll struck her so hard she doubled over, nearly collapsing. Every fiber of her being urged her to reveal the scroll from its hiding place and to read it.

But why? Simply to buy time? Lorna had already tried and failed to read the unfamiliar characters. It would be no different now.

Still, she couldn't resist the pull. Reaching into her robes, she pulled the silk scroll free and unrolled it, her eyes shifting to her sister.

Ereda scoffed. "Another one of your useless scrolls?" she barked, but all the same, she curled her fingers into a fist, and the shadow fiends paused in their slow descent toward Lorna.

Lorna gazed down at the scroll. The rune on her hand pulsed–not with pain, but with a gentle magic that seemed to travel from the brand up her arm, through her shoulder and spine, and ignite in her mind's eye.

The hieroglyphs suddenly revealed their meanings to her. Not all of them, but enough. Enough that a shadow of a smile crossed her lips, and she said, "Wait! You need not unleash this blood magic in the Realms. It will be your ruin. There is another way. A cleaner way. Let me show you."

The shadow empress growled out a deep, throaty laugh as if the words Lorna spoke were the most amusing things she had heard in all her long days. The laughter bounced off the walls, then faded once again into a quiet so pervasive that every breath Lorna took seemed to hang in the air.

The sneer on Ereda's face shifted, her expression becoming as blank and inscrutible as the carved stone statues that towered on either side of the massive onyx throne upon which she was perched.

Lorna took a deep breath and prayed her words would take root in her sister's mind and blossom into salvation. Ereda's preoccupation with the Elves, her desperation to conquer them and learn the ways of their magic, might just be the double-edged sword that could save her now.

She straightened, her gaze connecting with her sister's. Willing her voice not to shake but hearing it quaver anyway, she said, "This prophecy here reveals that I am touched by fate. The elf in the dungeons also said as much. There is only one who can bring the unity you crave to the realms; only one can bring all the fae and elves to heel. The Legion Queen. And without me, you cannot get to her. Without her, all your plans will unravel. If you kill me, whatever destiny is written in this scroll dies with me. If my star is extinguished, the paths connecting this destiny to yours will be closed to you."

Was it the truth? Lorna wasn't sure. She had read about the elven diviners who could read the future in the twinkling of the night sky. But the words she spoke were pure conjecture. Would fate find another string to weave into its designs for the future if one line was cut? Or did the whole pattern unravel?

The elves might know, but Lorna did not.

Still, she held the scroll out to Ereda like an olive branch. Her fingers brushed the soft, smooth surface. Again, the symbols were illuminated in gold with her touch. Lorna's heartbeat quickened as her sister studied the document with pursed lips. She knew her very life dangled from this tiny sliver of hope. If Ereda believed Lorna still had a role to play, a necessary one, perhaps she would call off her shadow fiends and let her live.

And despite all the hardships in her life, Lorna did not want her magic to go out. She wasn't ready for the Void. Thoughts of Osiris flitted through her mind as Ereda examined the scroll. Would her first kiss be her last?

The empress looked up. The expression on Ereda's face was not kind. Her eyes were narrowed to slits, her lips pulled down in a deep scowl that cut sharp lines of dismay into her forehead.

Yet, instead of urging the shadow fiends on, she waved her hand in the air, and the beasts began to evaporate with the motion. The congealed dark matter dispersed, whisking back to the corners of the throne room to hover around the glowing torches.

"Very well," Ereda said.

Lorna's heart stuttered in her chest, and she felt the burn of relieved tears sting her eyes, tracing cool paths down her burning cheeks.

"Thank you, sister," she whispered.

A long silence stretched in the room. The only sound was their breathing and the sputtering flames in the candelabras. Lorna dared not speak, and Ereda seemed inclined not to.

It was Bleakhart who finally broke the stillness. "Your Majesty, surely there must be some punishment for defying—" he began.

Ereda whipped her head around and speared the old sorcerer with a withering look, the snakes in her hair hissing.

"Did I ask for your opinion, mongrel?" she growled.

The loose skin of Bleakhart's jowls pulled tight against the jagged bones of his face as he gave the empress a cursory bow.

"My apologies, Your Majesty. I only thought–"

Ereda silenced him with another chilling glare and then redirected her attention to Lorna, who remained crouched on the floor at her sister's feet.

"Stand," Ereda ordered.

Lorna obeyed, though her legs trembled and scarcely felt capable of holding her.

"I will spare you, but Bleakhart is right," the Shadow empress assessed. "Your insolence cannot go completely unpunished."

With her sister's words, the relief that had washed over Lorna with the dismissal of the shadow fiends flagged. She looked up at Ereda, her lavender eyes haunted, and said, "Sister, I swear to you, I will never betray you again."

The empress scoffed at the words, then began to pace, her heels clicking a staccato rhythm on the black floor like a clock ticking down to an explosion. She drew to a stop in front of Lorna and looked her up and down with a smirk.

"Sister?"

Lorna tried to catch Ereda's eye with her pleading gaze, but her sister looked past her toward something in the back of the room.

"Guard," the empress bellowed, and the doors in the rear of the throne room opened. "Bring me Osiris Bane."

The guard didn't speak in answer, and with her back to him, Lorna could not see him stride from the room. But she heard the thud of his heavy plate boots and the shriek of the massive door's hinges. She flinched at the sound of it banging shut, her head buzzing and flashes of white light speckling her vision.

She had made a mistake.

She should have let the shadow fiends devour her.

For whatever Ereda had planned, it was surely far worse. If Ereda wanted to inflict physical pain on Lorna, she would have had Bleakhart punish her. The sorcerer was old and frail, but he was a practiced torturer. His methods elicited chilling screams, even from the elven captives, a race known for their stoicism.

That she had sent for Osiris meant that this punishment was something else entirely.

There could only be one reason why the empress had summoned her emissary. She knew of their repressed feelings. But how? And how much did she know? Had Ereda somehow found out about the stolen kiss? Or was it just that she had witnessed Osiris's ceaseless doting on Lorna over the years and his flirting, the pursuit that Lorna had so desperately tried to put an end to for this very reason?

Anyone Lorna got close to could be a weapon in her sister's hands.

At the sound of the door's wail, Lorna turned her head to see Osiris escorted into the room by two guards. He stood tall and appeared completely unconcerned. However, when he noticed Lorna kneeling on the floor, his posture went rigid, and his jaw muscle ticked.

Lorna turned back to her sister. "What are you going to do?" she asked in a small, quivering voice.

Ereda's eyebrows rose. "What makes you think *I'm* going to do anything?"

The smug expression on her sister's face and the cold gleam in her eye told Lorna everything she needed to know. Whatever Ereda had in mind, it would be a misery beyond simple pain.

The shadow empress cut her gaze to Osiris, and something new sparked in her sister's eyes, something Lorna had never seen in Ereda before, as she assessed her emissary.

Lust.

Ereda desired Osiris.

And Lorna could see why. Osiris was not in uniform but wore a loose gray tunic unlaced to his navel like he'd simply pulled it over his head and come running to heed Ereda's summon. Black leather riding pants were slung low on his hips, the tunic tucked into them to reveal his muscular thighs, the corded muscles of his abdomen visible through the thin fabric. His hair was loose and damp, like he'd just come from the baths, and his eyes shone in the torchlight—confident but appraising.

Ereda's tongue slid across her lower lip, and she smiled slightly as she took in Osiris's countenance.

Lorna felt a pang of jealousy she knew she had no right to as Osiris smiled uneasily back at her sister, his innate charm turned on.

"Osiris will be the one meting out your punishment."

Lorna's breath escaped her lips in a hiss. Alarm flashed in Osiris's eyes as they met Lorna's briefly before returning to Ereda, his expression mastered once more. But no doubt, the empress had witnessed the flicker of panic. She knew exactly what she was doing.

Ereda waved her hand in the air, and shadows flocked to it, spinning with dark energy and forging themselves into a long, thin whip. The conjuration grew a barbed head in the image of a cobra, mouth open and ready to strike. Unfurling the arcane lash, its length trail to the floor at her feet, she held the weapon out to Osiris.

"Show my sister what happens when you disobey me," Ereda ordered in an icy tone.

Osiris's lips curled back in a grimace, unable to hide

his dismay. Lorna had never seen him lose control of his countenance so completely.

His eyes flashed to Bleakhart as he said, "Perhaps you should have the mutt sorcerer do it. Torture and beatings are more his area of expertise than mine. I'm afraid I wouldn't know the first thing about how to use that thing." He indicated the whip with a tilt of his head, his nose wrinkling in disgust.

Ereda cracked the whip with a *snap* that ricocheted off the stone walls of the throne room, loud as thunder. "Are you defying me too, Bane?"

Osiris deflated, his shoulders slumping as his gaze met Lorna's once again. The beginnings of tears might have sparkled there—or perhaps it was just a trick of the light. Lorna couldn't be sure.

When Osiris broke off the eye contact, not to look at Ereda but at the floor as he took the offered weapon. "I'm sorry." Whether the apology was to Lorna or Ereda was unclear, but his voice cracked as he uttered it.

A single tear slipped past the dam of Lorna's will. She wiped it away and choked out, "Just do what she tells you, Osiris."

Ignoring her sister, Ereda barked, "Stand and remove your robes, Lorna."

Following her own advice, Lorna did as she was told. No good could come from fighting the empress; it would only serve to make things worse. She left the scroll lying at her feet and stood, unfastening the lacing of her bodice with trembling fingers. The garment fell to the throne room floor in a black puddle at her feet, leaving her standing, naked as the day she was born, her black wings held tight at her shoulders, trembling.

"Turn around," Ereda ordered.

The cool air prickled Lorna's exposed skin, and she shivered, wrapping her arms around her shoulders to hide her peaked nipples.

"Thank you for obeying. Now, whip her."

Lorna's back was to Osiris, but she craned her neck to look over her shoulder at him as he hefted the whip to get a feel for it. Three feet of thick leather uncoiled, the snake's head cracker the size of a fist hitting the ground. Osiris was dead-eyed and tight-lipped as he stared down at the bullwhip. All color drained from his sepia skin, leaving him ashen and drawn.

He cast a sidelong glance at Ereda as if he thought this might be a cruel trick to teach them a lesson. But if Osiris thought the empress might have a change of heart, Lorna knew better. To sway from her chosen path now would make her appear weak. And Ereda would never allow herself to be seen as weak.

The shadow empress's expression was one of grim determination, her dark eyes hard as iron as she nodded sharply at Osiris. "Go ahead. What are you waiting for? I said, hit her."

"Osiris, just do it," Lorna begged. She couldn't stand to see him punished for her transgressions too. And she knew Ereda would do just that; she was probably even looking forward to it.

Osiris hesitated, giving Arianette a pained look before raising the whip and flicking it. The practice shot stirred the air near Lorna's face, the breeze it left in its wake cooling her hot, tear-splashed cheeks.

"I'm sorry, Lorna," he whispered again, and this time there could be no doubt the apology was meant for her.

Lorna wished he hadn't said it. The pain in his voice made what was coming even harder for her to bear.

"It's not your fault, Osiris. You owe me no apologies," she murmured, then turned away, squaring her shoulders and staring straight ahead at the massive throne room doors and the two shadow fae guards looking on with cool indifference to the proceedings.

Then the hiss of the whip slicing the air sounded.

For a moment, there was nothing, then it hit Lorna's back with a crack and a sting that took her breath away. She gasped, her whole body instinctively flinching away from the impact of the knotted cracker. But still, she refused to give her sister the satisfaction of seeing her cry.

"Again," Ereda snarled behind her. "And this time, hit her like the traitor she is, not like your lover." Lorna could hear the jealousy in her sister's voice. Yes, she had defied her and refused to help Bleakhart interrogate the elves. But this was about more than that.

Osiris's exhalation was a strangled, broken thing. Somewhere off to the side came a sound that could have been one of Bleakhart's wet coughs or stifled laughter.

Lorna's back throbbed in a strip from her left shoulder to her hip, but Ereda wasn't done yet.

The fleeting thought that she wished her sister was right and Osiris was her lover flashed through her mind. What sweetness had she let pass her by out of fear of the very thing happening to her right now? She had done nothing but prolong her misery. The end result was the same.

"Ereda, she is bleeding. Surely whatever she has done—"

"Do it!" Ereda boomed.

Osiris only grunted in reply.

The next blow came, twice as hard as the first. It stung like a hot razor, and Lorna heard the rip as the snake's head sheared through her flesh, stripping ribbons of it away from her spine. Something warm and wet— her blood?—dripped down her lower back.

Lorna doubled over, her stomach heaving from the pain, threatening to spill, stars flashing in her vision. She righted herself, straightening once more, just as Ereda said: "That's better. Again. Harder."

"You'll kill her."

The certainty in Osiris's words struck home, and Lorna could hold her tears back no longer, and they broke free, streaming down her cheeks as she let out a plaintive wail. This time the sound from the side of the room was unmistakably Bleakhart's laughter.

She knotted her fingers in the prayer position and prayed for the Xennia's strength. *Please Goddess, if you are real, if ever you have watched over me, please spare me. I am not ready for the void.*

With her silent words, the rune on Lorna's palm pulsed, filling her with warmth and numbness. The strangest sensation came over her, almost as if her mind was detached from her body, floating somewhere amorphous, near but not here. Similar to

When the whip made contact the third time. Lorna's

wings moved on reflex to block the blow, and when it landed, she felt the delicate, hollow bones shatter. The thin, membranous black skin shredded, and there was a brief moment of pain so pure and intense Lorna could not name or describe the agony.

But it only lasted an instant. Then all feeling, all sensation, all thoughts were gone.

Her lavender eyes flew open, and she saw herself prone on the throne room floor as if from a great height. She wondered if the blow had snapped vertebrae and killed her.

Then the world went dark, and Lorna thought no more.

No Fight Left

Lorna tried to open her eyes, but her lids fluttered closed again. Her body felt like dead weight, something detached from her, unwilling to obey her commands. Heavy and aching, broken and torn. Even breathing was difficult. Like she was once again being held beneath the lapping waters of the blood pools, asphyxiated by her sister.

Where am I?

She tried desperately to get her bearings. The room was warm, and the bed beneath her soft. Was it her own bed? No. Her simple, utilitarian bed was not nearly so luxurious. And the scent on the sheets... not hers, but familiar. Comforting.

Whose?

A cloth pressed against her desiccated back, cool but burning with an intensity that took her breath away with the initial contact... then soothing. Tender, like the fingers that brushed across her brow.

Through the haze, she heard whispers, words she couldn't make out, but they were gentle, almost loving.

Whose?

Where am I? Why do I hurt so badly?

Lorna tried to ask these very questions, but the words refused to come. So she forced her thoughts to collect in the miasma of confusion and anguish.

The whipping.

It came back to her in a flash. Osiris Bane, wielding her sister's wicked weapon. Ereda had not cared if she died—had, perhaps, wanted to kill her.

And Lorna had though it was all over. Thought she would return to the Void and meet her maker on this day.

Did I survive? But how. I was floating, no longer in my body.

But she knew she must have, or else she would not be here—wherever here was. Perhaps it would have been better if she had died...the pain...so intense. Excruciating on a level she had not imagined possible. Then a faint tingle of warmth in her palm, a pulse of magic. Not her own, strange to her, but from within her, relief flowed, easing it only a little.

Then the cloth pressed against her back again, and fresh pain made her grind her teeth until she thought they might splinter. When it faded, Lorna slept.

Minutes, days, hours. Lorna would never know how long she remained cocooned in the sweet relief that was sleep. But when she woke again, the pain had eased marginally. Enough that she could, at least, breathe. Her eyes flew open, finally heeding her mind's commands, darting wildly around the space. Black tapestries depicting the Wild Hunt hung on the walls. Not the same walls as her room. These walls were simple gray stone, not the obsidian of the royal tower. She was somewhere else.

Blue-flamed torches burned around her, casting shadows. That was all she could make out before the pain came again, and she squeezed her eyes closed against it, willing it away. Lorna attempted to steady her thoughts and piece things together when it passed. Neither her room nor her sister's. Certainly not Bleakhart's dungeon.

Where am I?

She tried to roll over to get a better view, but a white-hot shockwave lanced through her body, bringing stinging tears to her eyes. Then a hand on her cheek, wiping away the dampness of her spilled tears.

Whose?

"Easy, love. Be easy. Try not to move too much." She knew the voice. Gruff and choked with emotion, but familiar.

Love?

Who? No one here loves me. I am alone in this miserable world. Alone and despised.

Lorna struggled to grasp the mystery, to find the answer to that simple question, but her thoughts were foggy and would not connect. Trying to force them only made her head ache and join the symphony of pain playing throughout her body.

But she had to know.

Where am I? And am I safe here? Had she survived Ereda's assault only to languish in agony until her sister returned to strike the killing blow? Was this respite merely a way to prolong her misery?

With what felt like a heroic effort, Lorna turned her head to the side just enough to see who sat beside her. And at the sight of him, despite it all, she smiled.

"Oh, it's you," she whispered, lifting a shaking hand to cup his cheek.

Osiris.

His black hair hung loose, framing a haggard face with red-rimmed eyes. He'd been crying. But why? This wasn't his fault. It was hers. If she had just done what Bleakhart had told her to. If she hadn't contradicted Ereda in the throne room. If she'd done a better job of hiding her feelings for him. There were a thousand things Lorna wished she could do differently to spare them both this misery.

"I'm sorry," she whispered.

Osiris shook his head in disbelief, taking her hand in his and giving it the gentlest possible squeeze.

"You amaze me, Lorna Blackburn," he whispered, lowering his head and pressing his lips against her ear as he spoke. "Here you are, broken and bleeding, by my hand, and me without a cut. And you're apologizing to me? There's nothing to be sorry for, beautiful girl. I'm the one who is sorry."

Osiris trailed his lips from her ear up her cheekbone, then to her forehead, planting a lingering kiss there.

Lorna wanted to tell him he was wrong. That this was her doing. She wanted to tell him to stop tending to her and to leave her be. The two of them together could only end up in more trouble now that Ereda knew they cared for one another.

But she was so weary, so sore. No fight left in her. And it felt so good to be touched with a kind hand and cared for.

Her eyelids grew heavy again and drooped. Then she drifted of to sleep once more.

Vague remembrances—fever dreams or memories? Osiris, holding her hand and whispered to her while she screamed, the pain too much for her to bear. Had she imagined that? Lorna wasn't sure. Her thoughts were still clouded when she woke in the room once more.

She blinked and pushed herself to sit up, wincing, and clenched her teeth to keep from crying. The pain of the lacerations running the length of her back and her tattered wings was certainly still present and very real.

How long had she drifted in and out of consciousness, delirious?

Lorna had no idea. She remembered Osiris tending her. But now, that recollection shot a stab of pain through her. Ereda would not have released her to Osiris's care. She was putting him, in even more danger.

A narrow window across the room allowed a view of a courtyard she had never seen before. She tried to figure out where she was to determine the best means of escape before Osiris returned. Outside, the sky was burnt orange as the sun sank, but the mountains...where were the mountains? If she fled—

But no. She could not fly over the Funeral Mountains. Her wings were broken, and besides, all that she would find there was another prison.

Lorna rubbed her temples, a strange buzz in her head. Had she been drugged? Maybe to ease the pain. She took a deep breath. Trophies hung from the walls, deep ebony and gleaming onyx carvings in the shapes of different creatures. A unicorn. A bear. A buck.

Awards from the Wild Hunt, Lorna realized, furrowing her brow.

She had never cared for the hunt. Too many were injured, sometimes killed. Not only animals were tracked, captured, enslaved, and sometimes slaughtered. Fae who had committed crimes, spies from other Courts, and duels between rivals were all settled with a Hunt. It served as a means of disposing of unsavory elements, culling over-population—of animals and lesser fae—entertaining the masses and solving disputes. Many prominent positions in the Court were earned by participants of middling bloodlines who would have had difficulty climbing the rungs on the ladder to prestige without participating in the sordid event.

The ladder. Osiris.

He had no link to the Blackburn bloodline, but he'd first won his position as a page in the Shadow Court by competing in the Hunt when he was barely more than a boy. And from there, he kept competing and continued climbing until, finally, he was promoted to Ereda's emissary.

Her brain clicked slowly, struggling to make the connection between the Hunt trophies, her battered body, and this strange room.

Finally, it registered.

The fool brought me to his own home.

Panic fluttered like a hundred moths pounding their wings in Lorna's belly, moving up to her chest, hastening the beating of her heart.

She shouldn't be here. How had Osiris managed to get her to his chambers, and how long had she been gone? There was no chance Ereda had just let Osiris walk out with her cradled in his arms. He must have somehow taken her.

Lorna didn't have time to puzzle it out.

She pushed herself upright and threw her legs over the side of the bed to flee. She had to leave before Ereda found her—them— and did something even more cruel and terrible than what she'd already done.

Her feet hit the floor, and she struggled to rise, but the wounds on her back tore open anew with the motion. She tried to bite back the strangled scream before it left her throat but failed.

No faster had the sound left her lips than Osiris appeared in the doorway.

"Lorna! What in the Goddess's name are you doing? Get back in bed."

Lorna would have laughed at the chiding, mother-hen tone coming from the tall, muscular man, who hastened across the room toward her if the situation had been less dire.

He was dripping wet—evidently, her cry had interrupted a bath—and wore nothing but a robe, open to his hips. Soaking wet hair hung loose, and droplets of water beaded in the trail of wiry hair running from his chest to his navel.

His image took her breath away, and she struggled to block out memories of that fleeting kiss in her bedroom, which had likely doomed them both. She stared at him and forced herself to say, "Osiris, why did you bring me here? How? Don't you know Ereda–"

Osiris was at Lorna's side before she could finish the sentence.

"Lorna, I have a plan. A plan so that Ereda won't hurt you again. Ever. I promise."

"A plan?" Lorna echoed dully.

If Osiris thought his words would bring Lorna comfort, he could not have been more wrong. She tried to remain standing, but everything hurt, and when Osiris reached her side and guided her to sit with hands on her shoulders, she could not refuse the gentle touch of his cool fingers against her still-fevered skin.

She sat on the bed and gazed at him, waiting for an explanation she was terrified to hear.

"A plan," he repeated, with a devious look in his eye. "But first, you have to heal."

Lorna blinked at Osiris and shook her head, confused. "Does she know I'm here?"

"No," he said simply, "and she won't, at least not for a while."

Lorna's brow furrowed in confusion. How could Ereda not know her whereabouts? Her sister kept tabs on her every waking moment. Lorna suspected all the palace guards reported her every move back to the empress whenever she left her chambers in the tower.

"I don't think you understand. My sister—" Lorna started, but Osiris stopped her, bringing his finger to her lips and pressing it to them.

"Shhh. Let me explain."

Too weary to protest further, Lorna gave a slight nod of acquiescence. Osiris removed his finger and swept her tangled dark hair behind her ears, giving her a kind smile that made her heart squeeze. She licked her lips, tasting the faint saltiness left behind by his touch and her tears.

"Ereda wanted you banished to the dungeons immediately, but I convinced Bleakhart to give me a few hours to tend to your wounds. I informed him that, no matter how angry the empress was, she would not be pleased if her sister died in his care without a direct order and that he could expect a worse punishment than what you had endured should it happen. The man is a fine torturer but not much of a healer, so he relented when I put it that way."

Osiris's smile curled into a smirk as Lorna studied him, narrowing her eyes. "But if he knows I'm with you, he'll be back..."

Osiris chuckled and shook his head. "Do you really

think I've risen from nothing to become the empress's emissary by being a fool?"

His hands moved to Lorna's shoulders, and he gave them an ever-so-gentle reassuring squeeze. She wanted to curl into that touch, lean her head against his chest, and just trust that he was doing what was best. But she couldn't.

"So how will you keep Bleakhart away?" she asked.

Osiris gave a dismissive wave of his hand. "Bleakhart has already come and gone. I sent another girl with him in your stead."

He said it with a winning smile and such confidence, but Lorna's stomach turned with the words, and her ears began to ring. *Another girl? Who? And what will become of them?*

When she didn't answer and only stared at him blankly with something like horror written on her face, Osiris quickly went on. "She looked enough like you to pass, and her family was well compensated. I didn't beat her badly, only enough to leave marks that would be believable, and gave her poppy flower to numb the–"

Lorna couldn't believe what she was hearing. Her head swam, and she felt light-headed. Reaching up to wrench Osiris's hands from her shoulders, she forced out, "You sent an innocent girl to endure my punishment? You beat her with a whip?"

Osiris's mouth hung open, startled at Lorna's response. But what had he expected? For her to graciously thank him for sending another to their doom in her place?

"Osiris, you must undo what you've done," Lorna

begged. "Whoever the girl is, get her back from Bleakhart and send her back to her family. She doesn't deserve—"

Osiris's eyes went hard as flint. "No. I won't do it."

"Please," Lorna pleaded, "I could never live with myself knowing—"

Osiris snatched up Lorna's hands and squeezed them with clear possessiveness. "No. She knew what she was agreeing to. She did it by choice to give her family a better life. With the coin I've paid them, they'll be comfortable until the end of their days. And I can't—I won't—see you hurt again. Not by Bleakhart, not by Ereda, not by anyone."

Tears sprang to Lorna's eyes at the earnest urgency in his tone. Osiris thought he was helping her—saving her, even. But how could she ever live with herself, knowing another was suffering for her crimes and failings? Worse, the ruse could not last for long, and when it was found, all three of them would suffer unimaginable consequences.

She choked back a sob and said, "Osiris, Ereda will know that girl isn't me. I'm her sister, for Xennia's sake. And when she finds out what you've done—"

Osiris scoffed. "By the time Ereda finds out, we will be long gone. Far away and untouchable," he assured her.

"What are you talking about?" Lorna whispered.

As much as she did not want to feel relief, she did, as a tiny flame of hope kindled in her chest. To leave the Shadow Court with Osiris...but it didn't take long for doubt to needle her with sharp claws. Where could they possibly go that would put them outside Ereda's clutches?

As if reading her mind, Osiris said, "I've sent a message to Lord Skyborn requesting sanctuary. He has agreed to hear our case. Lorna"—he released his grip on her hands, taking her chin between his and cradling her face, drawing her gaze to meet his—"we are going to the Court of Sky."

We Fly At Dawn

A chill started at the base of Lorna's spine and crept up every vertebra in her ravaged back. The Court of Sky? Enemies of the Shadow fae since time immemorial?

She stared at Osiris, her expression blank. "Have you gone mad? Is this a cruel joke?"

Of all the places in the Realms, was Osiris truly suggesting that the safest place for her, the sister of the Shadow Empress, and him, a member of the upper echelon of the Shadow Court, was in the hands of their lifelong enemies?

"Listen to me, Lorna." Osiris's expression was somber, his eyes flashing with something Lorna could not name. Fear? Conviction? "War is coming."

Lorna rolled her eyes. "We're already at war with the

elves. We have been for hundreds of years. Do you think I haven't been reminded of it every day of my whole life?"

"No!" Osiris boomed, slapping his palms down on his thighs.

Lorna flinched back from the unexpected burst of emotion. The sharp sting of her wounds reopening with the sudden motion made her hiss and grind her teeth. But Osiris didn't pause to comfort her this time.

"This is more than that," he went on in a hushed but urgent voice. "I'm not talking about this long, drawn-out war of attrition we've been fighting with the elves for centuries. This is something different."

Lorna's heart thudded dully in her chest, and the rune on her palm pulsed. Almost as if it was warning her that Osiris was right... something was coming. Something terrible.

"What are you talking about?" she whispered.

Osiris's jaw muscle ticked, and this time there was no questioning that what she saw in his eyes was fear.

"When Ereda holds her Reckoning, she will give all the courts a choice. Unite with her in her mission to defeat the elves, the mortals, and the Dreamers once and for all...or be destroyed."

Lorna's head buzzed. A war amongst the fae? There had always been bitter rivalries, but an all-out war? It was unheard of. The casualties...

Osiris's voice softened, and he leaned in close to Lorna, interrupting the spiral of her thoughts. "I know you cannot do what Ereda will ask you to do in the days ahead. It would break you. Even if she forgave your most recent transgression, Bleakhart would ask the unthinkable of you, and you'd be back in that throne room, deemed a traitor, and this time there would be no escape for you. She would have your head."

Loath as Lorna was to admit it, she knew Osiris was right. Ereda had already proven that she did not care for her beyond what she could provide to help her wage her war. The Shadow empress would push Bleakhart to pursue his blood magic-infused experiments even more zealously, with the elves and the Dream fae as her sworn energy—and force Lorna to aid him.

And what of the Courts of Sky and Sea? They would be fools to think they could stand against Ereda's martial might alone—but with the power of the elves at their back...would they, too, declare war?

Lorna rubbed her temples, trying to collect her thoughts. Finally, she settled on, "And what makes you think the Sky fae will have us, given who we are?"

"Lord Vargas has given me his word. I have met with him many times as an envoy. We respect one another, the enmity between our courts aside. He will grant us asylum for as long as we need it if we come to him. All he asks is your help with some translations and mine as a messenger between Sky and Dreams."

Lorna pursed her lips, trying to think. She wasn't convinced. Just because a promise was made didn't mean it would be kept—unless it was bound with a geis. And surely Osiris would have mentioned it if his pact with the Skylord was bound I'm such a way.

They could reach the Sky Court and be held captive —ransomed back to Ereda. They would be valuable hostages. Her sister's fury at their desertion alone would convince her to strike a hard bargain to get them back—if only to torture and kill them herself.

But what choice did they have?

"You were a fool to bring me here," Lorna chided Osiris, but there was no anger in her tone, only weariness and resignation. "You should have left me to rot in the Undercity. Now both our lives are ruined."

Fast as a shadow cat, Osiris was on her, his face close to hers, so close that she could smell the cinnamon and clove scent of his breath. Careful not to touch her wounded back, Osiris gripped her by the shoulders.

"This is not the end for us, Lorna. I swear it. It's a new beginning. I have plans ready. We fly at dawn. Will you come away with me and find a life where we can truly be free?"

That flicker of hope returned in Lorna's chest, sparking along with the rune on her palm, guiding her.

An ember that she refused to fan, yet all the same. With an almost imperceptible nod, Lorna Blackburn said, "All right, Osiris Bane. We fly at dawn."

After Osiris spoke, the absurdity of his words hit Lorna like a dagger to the heart. Testing her suspicion, she tried to stretch her wings and was overcome by a pain so intense it brought stars to her eyes and forced her to double over and breathe deep to keep from retching. If she had anything at all in h her stomach, she would have vomited it on the plush gray carpeted floor.

Fly at dawn?

She could not fly at all.

"Shhhh, stop. Don't do that." Osiris rubbed Lorna's

forearms as she hunched over, the touch soothing. "I have someone coming to help. By morning, the pain will be gone," he assured her.

Lorna let out a bark of bitter laughter and shook her head, wincing, eyes still fixed on the floor. "These wounds can't be healed in an evening, Osiris. And if someone has convinced you they can be, you've fallen for the ploy of a charlatan."

Osiris's hands stopped moving. Lorna wrenched herself upright again and saw a flicker of anger in his dark eyes.

"All this, and you still underestimate me, just as you always have." There was an edge to his voice that made a little shudder run through him, something hard Lorna did not know was in him. "Even when we were children, you did it, going out of your way to ignore me, though you've always felt the same way I feel about you. I knew it. I've known it since you were a girl. Why do you think I've done all that I have? The wild hunts, the climb. To show you, I may not be of your station, but I can and will do what needs to be done. To prove myself worthy of being with you."

Lorna cringed. When he put it like that, it made her sound cruel. He wasn't entirely wrong, but he didn't understand. She hadn't been that way to be cruel but to protect him. "Osiris, I–"

Osiris's eyes snapped to hers, his gaze not just smoldering but blazing now. "Don't lie to me, Lorna. I know the way the world works. I'm not a fool. I did think that after how far I've come from a lowly nobody, and after all this"—he gestured in the air—"you might finally have a little faith–"

Before Osiris could finish, a knock sounded. Three quiet taps, then a louder one.

My sister comes. This was all for naught, Lorna thought, her heartbeat quickening.

But Osiris's expression had gone placid. The anger drained from his face, a tinge of a smile on his lips as he rose and crossed the room, opening the chamber door.

"Osiris!" Lorna called, not wanting him to leave her side, fearing what lurked beyond the safety of this room.

But it was not Ereda who stepped crossed the threshold. Instead, someone far taller and more slender, wrapped in a black cloak with the hood pulled low to conceal the wearer's features.

"Who–" Lorna started to ask, but Osiris reached up, lowering the hood to reveal delicate features and pale, faintly gray skin.

Lorna studied the woman's face, gasping in surprise. "I know you," she whispered.

"Amsa Coralline," the elf standing in Osiris Bane's doorway announced in a soft voice with a bow of her head and a knowing smile.

Coralline. The elf had touched Lorna in Bleakhart's dungeon and shown her the hand of fate in the stars.

Lorna shook her head and blinked as if the creature might be an illusion, a hallucination brought on by pain that would soon vanish. But when she opened her eyes again, Coralline was still there, standing beside Osiris.

"But how?" Lorna asked in confusion.

"Don't worry about that now. It's as I said; you

underestimate my reach in this court. Few doors are closed to me that I cannot unlock."

Osiris took the elf by the hand and led her to the bed, where she dropped down lightly beside Lorna.

"Shadow's sister," Coralline said in her lilting accent, "daughter who will bear the prophecy."

Lorna wanted to protest. No, she was neither of those things; the hated name, the frightening fate. But she was too stunned to find words as Coralline lifted Lorna's right hand and examined the rune etched into it.

"You already bear the cruceamena rune. My gift to you." The serenity in the elf's voice lulled Lorna into a feeling of deep calm as she gazed at the mark on her outstretched palm.

"What does it do?" Lorna asked.

Coralline traced the rune with a long, gnarled finger, and it ignited, glowing golden. The warmth she had felt in Ereda's throne room before the bizarre out-of-body experience that preceded her blackout filled her with the elf's touch.

The elf raised her eyes from the rune and studied Lorna, who squirmed beneath the intensity of her gaze. "Painbringer. When you call on it, the rune will turn your suffering into power." Coralline's fingers danced over Lorna's skin. Then stopped as she frowned and whispered, "And you have suffered much in your life."

Lorna's gaze dropped to the floor. How could this elf who had been tortured and chained in the dungeon think *she*, the empress's sister, had suffered? She was mortified to even think it. Lorna had lived a life of privilege. Until today, no one had ever hurt her or kept her captive.

As if reading her thoughts, Coralline let Lorna's hand fall and whispered, "There are other kinds of captivity than mine, and wounds inflicted with words can be as painful as the sting of the whip."

Was it true, Lorna wondered? Had her life of servitude been as much a misery as this poor slave's?

Lorna didn't have time to consider because Coralline continued, "I can show you how to harness the power of everything that has ever hurt you and use it to heal if you'll let me. Will you?"

Their gazes connected, and in the fathomless depths of Coralline's eyes, Lorna saw no malice, only a deep love and light that made her feel strangely at peace. She whispered, "Show me how."

"Close your eyes, sister," the elf whispered, and Lorna did. "Now think about what pains you, the wounds you wish to feel. You must embrace it. Understand that while it hurts, it will make you stronger. Your pain is part of what makes you who you are, but you are more than your pain. And with the rune, you have the power to control it."

The idea of acknowledging the fiery, burning lash marks and flayed skin made Lorna's hands clam up, and her throat tighten. She closed her eyes, but when she tried to focus, her thoughts scattered, seeking any escape from the misery. She couldn't do it. It was too hard. Like her sister had always said, she was weak. Pathetic.

With a gentle touch on her forearm, Coralline said,

"Trust me, sister. Be brave. This is your path to freedom. A way to break your chains."

Was it, though, Lorna wondered? Or was she only trading Ereda's prison for another in the Court of Sky? An unfamiliar world inhabited by fae who had been her people's enemies for centuries. Would they ever truly accept her there?

Which was worse, the monster she knew or the one that might lie in wait in a distant castle in the clouds?

"Lorna, please. Please, just try." Osiris's voice shattered her stream of consciousness.

For a moment, she had forgotten. If she stayed, Osiris would suffer too. Ereda would subject them *both* to exquisite torture for defying and betraying her. Again she lamented that he had even brought her here. Osiris should have left her in the dungeons where she belonged.

But he hadn't, and after all he had done to save her, she had to at least try.

Lorna took a deep, steadying breath. She twitched her wings and held them slightly extended, agony lancing through her. It was excruciating, unlike anything she had ever felt before.

"More," Coralline whispered.

It seemed impossible. Already, Lorna's head was light, and her stomach churned, threatening to expel whatever meager contents remained. But she had to try. If not for herself, for Osiris.

She flexed her membranous black wings again, spreading them wider, feeling the scabs peel back and small rivers of warm blood flow down her back.

This time, she nearly swooned, her head dropping

into her lap as she hunched over. A strangled cry that turned into a long moan escaped her lips despite her best efforts to bite it back.

She couldn't stand it. The pain was too much, and as it overwhelmed her, Lorna prayed Xennia would claim her for the void just to spare her.

But then something strange happened. Lorna felt the rune on her hand heat, its warmth radiating from the tips of her fingers to the crown of her head, much as it had during the whipping. The pain was still there, but it felt removed. A small thing, like a shadow wisp that won't be shooed away, but hovers, niggling and buzzing, waiting for the right moment to bite.

When Coralline spoke, she sounded like she was very far away, yet whispering right into Lorna's ear at the same time.

"Do you feel the Elven magic? Already, it is trying to fight the pain. Acknowledge it. Embrace it, and let it move through you, a river of gold flowing through your veins."

Lorna tried to give the strange new magic her full attention. It was like pure light. So clean, pure, and bright that she wondered how it could even coexist with her own shadow magic. On and on it went, pouring into her, the vessel.

And suddenly, she realized she felt no pain whatsoever anymore.

Her eyes flew open in surprise to find Coralline and Osiris staring at her.

"Stretch your wings," Coralline said with a nod and a wistful smile.

And Lorna did, opening them to their full span and gasping in wonder.

No pain.

Lorna was healed.

Could it be, Lorna wondered. Was she truly healed? It seemed impossible. How could such magic exist... not only exist, but be wielded by the likes of her?

Lorna rose, spreading her wings to their full span. As she did so, she felt a slight strain—the dull ache of scar tissue stretching, but still, there was no pain whatsoever.

"Am I really healed?" she murmured in astonishment.

Osiris came up beside her, and, with the gentlest possible touch, turned her around. His fingers traced her back between the roots of her wings, and Lorna heard him gasp, then murmur, "Amazing. I've never seen anything like it."

"You see what you can do, sister? You have more power than you know," came Coralline's quiet, melodic voice.

Lorna turned to look at her and blushed. "It is only the rune. I could never—"

Now Coralline crossed the space between them, reached out, and took Lorna by the shoulders, shaking her a little roughly. "No. It isn't only the rune. All the rune does is channel the power within *you*. If you had no power, the rune would do nothing. That is the secret of Elven magic."

Lorna wanted to deny it. She had spent her entire life feeling powerless, after all. How could it be that *she* had the power to heal, as she'd just done?

She didn't know what to say as she looked from Coralline to Osiris, swallowing hard, words unwilling to form as the tears in her eyes changed from anguish and fear to joy.

Coralline spared her from having to find words by speaking. "You must both go. The hour grows late. Dawn will be here before you know it."

"But what about you?" Lorna asked, concerned.

This elven woman had saved her life. Where would she go now? How would she escape without being caught by Ereda and dragged back to the dungeons? The idea sent a shudder rolling through Lorna. She couldn't stand to see that happen.

Coralline gave Lorna a strange look, and something that could only be described as mischief sparkled in her bright eyes.

"Do not worry about me, Shadow's sister," the elf said.

Lorna wanted to protest—how could she not worry? This woman had saved her life—but the words died on her lips. In the span of a blink, the tall, slender elf was gone.

At first, Lorna thought she had disappeared, perhaps using something like a shadow cloak, until she heard soft scuffling. She looked down to see a small gray field mouse scamper across the floor, then slip through the space underneath the closed door and vanish.

Osiris chuckled. "I would not worry about her. I have a feeling she'll make it out of here all right."

A grin tugged at the corners of Lorna's lips—

goddess, it felt like it had been a hundred years since she had last smiled—but it didn't last long, for Osiris spoke.

"Come," he said, gesturing.

Lorna followed him across the room to the door Coralline had disappeared through, where Osiris removed two black cloaks from the hooks, slinging one over his shoulders, fitting his wings through the two slits in the back, and pulling the hood low on his face. The other he covered Lorna with, careful to be gentle with her newly healed back as he arranged the folds of fabric and freed her wings.

When he was done, he turned Lorna around and smiled at her. But she could see it was forced, and there was a flicker of fear in his dark eyes.

Lorna felt it too.

Whether or not they escaped the Court of Shadows without being discovered by her sister, everything would change for them from this point on. Life as they knew it was over, and the future was murky, the path unclear. What would the Sky Court hold if they even made it there? There was no way to know.

"Osiris." Lorna brought her hands to his cheeks, cradling his face. "Thank you," she whispered.

Then she leaned in. Osiris's eyes widened as Lorna's lips found his. The kiss was tender, sweet, and frustratingly brief, but even after she pulled away, the black pepper and cloves taste of his mouth lingered on her tongue.

When they pulled away, Osiris's eyes were dazed and half-lidded, his breath coming heavy. Twin flames of desire kindled in his eyes, and for a moment, Lorn thought he would take her, throw on his huge, soft bed, and ravage her right then and there.

And she wanted that.

Goddess, she wanted that desperately and had for a very long time, Lorna realized.

But there was no time, and at length, after a few rapid blinks, Osiris mastered her emotions. He took Lorna's hand in his and gave her a sad little smile.

"Come, beauty. It's time to fly."

What Tomorrow Will Bring

L orna stood on the balcony of Osiris's home in one of the tall black towers outside the gates of Castle Bleak. She gazed across the silver and jet of the Funeral Mountains, rising like sharp teeth gnawing on the horizon, dripping with the crimson of the rising sun.

She had never crossed those jagged, imposing peaks before. What lay beyond was, to her, another world. The Ethereal Realms were vast, yet Lorna had never been allowed to leave the small corner of the Shadow Court; beyond Castle Bleak, the world seemed foreign and terrifying.

But Osiris has been beyond the mountains, she reminded herself.

As Ereda's emissary, he had journeyed far and wide, seeing all the lands, from the crystal towers in Dream

Court to the Earth Court's metropolis buried deep in the heart of the earth. Osiris knew the way to the Court of Sky and would know the people there when they arrived. This gave her some comfort, though not much.

As Lorna stood lost in thought, the wind whipped her hood back and her long, dark hair caught in the wind. She let its cold fingers tangle in it and chill her skin. The wind. Dominion of the Court of Sky. Would she find a friend in it or just another enemy?

She felt a hand at the small of her back and turned to face Osiris.

"Remember, this is a beginning, not an end," he told Lorna, placing his hands on her shoulders and gazing deep into her eyes, steady and kind.

Lorna nodded, but as she did, a single tear escaped her eye and tracked down her cheek.

Since the day she was born, her life in the Shadow Court had been one of fear and servitude. Why, then, did the idea of leaving fill her with such emptiness? Why did she fear that the moment she stepped off this ledge and took to the sky, a cavern would open up inside her soul that would remain for all her days, never to be filled?

"I don't know why I'm so sad," Lorna admitted, leaning against Osiris's strong arm at her back and letting him support her.

Osiris traced the streak the tear had left, wiping it away, then smoothed Lorna's hair back, tucking it behind her ear.

He snaked his arm around Lorna's waist, pulling her to him, and told her, "It's okay to be afraid. Change is never easy."

A long sigh escaped Lorna's lips as she forced a smile she did not feel. The sense of dread, that feeling they were reaching for a future they could never hold, kept her lips tight. Was the deep foreboding a warning from fate? Or was it only in her mind?

She shook her head to clear it, but the cobwebs of malaise still clung, sticky in her thoughts.

"As long as I'm with you, I know it will be okay," she forced out, though she did not believe it.

Osiris kissed her forehead lightly, then pulled away, and Lorna instantly missed the heat of his body. He pulled her hood forward again, so her face was covered once more.

"The time is now," he told Lorna, spreading his black feathered wings.

Lorna did the same, the flesh of her back stinging only slightly as the fresh scar tissue puckered with the motion of the black leathery bat wings.

Osiris went first, vaulting into the sky.

Lorna hesitated only a moment, then she, too, was off.

The current caught her immediately, hoisting her into the sky and carrying her toward the imposing silhouettes of the mountains.

Lorna did not often fly, for where would she go? Now, as she coasted through the slate gray clouds, struggling to keep up with Osiris, it was immensely clear how much stronger he was than Lorna as his form pulled ahead. A sudden panic gripped her. What if he left her behind? She would get lost in the black peaks and shadowy valleys. Ereda and her guards would find her and...

But ahead, Osiris slowed, then came to a stop, turning back to look at Lorna as he hovered above the treeline.

He won't leave me, Lorna thought, bringing her panicked spiral to an end.

She pumped her wings harder and soon caught up. As they flew side by side, she heard Osiris call, "This is what it feels like to be alive," over the roar of the wind.

And an unexpected exhilaration filled Lorna as she realized he was right.

The jagged obsidian peaks shone below, sunlight reflecting off their gleaming surface. It would have been beautiful if the fear of being caught by one of Ereda's patrols had not cast its long shadow over Lorna's heart and mind.

Deep canyons cut into the rock face, and when they could, she and Osiris dipped into them to hide their presence as best as possible. Still, with every beat of her wings, the thought of soldiers breaking through the dense bank of slate-gray clouds, swooping down and carrying them away, back to her sister, haunted Lorna.

But as the hours passed and the wind carried them away from the Court of Shadows, none did. They flew unmolested, and overhead the skyscape gradually changed from gray to blue, the clouds scattering and turning to pale silver streaks. Below, the mountains became different too, rolling more gently, obsidian gradually shifting to pale crystalline gray and white.

As the sun began to sink behind them, painting this new and remarkable landscape in pink and gold, hope sprang in Lorna. They had crossed the border, leaving the Shadow Court behind them.

They had reached the Court of Sky.

Even the air smelled different as Lorna sucked in a deep breath. Colder but cleaner, without the underlying musk and decay.

Osiris swooped in close to her and said, "There are caves nearby. We'll rest there for the night. By tomorrow afternoon, we'll have reached the Sky Tower. Follow me."

Perhaps, Lorna thought. *But who knows what tomorrow will bring?*

The Flame She Was Drawn To

Lorna trailed Osiris as he led her east a few miles farther, then dropped on a low rock ledge. She hadn't realized how sore and weary she was from exertion, but when they stopped, she felt the dull ache in her wings and the prickling of the nerves on her freshly healed back.

Sensing her discomfort, Osiris walked up and wrapped his arms around her from behind. He embraced her for a moment, leaning his cheek against the crown of her head, then brought his hands to her shoulders, massaging the knots gently.

Lorna stiffened. It was strange, being touched like this. She had lived a life almost entirely devoid of touch, of connection, and now she found it strange and almost uncomfortable. But as Osiris worked to relieve the tension with deft fingers, she let herself relax.

"That feels good," she murmured.

"Good, that's all I want for you. To make you feel good. To make you happy."

Osiris reached up and pulled her hood down, running his fingers through the wind-swept tangles of her black hair. Lorna closed her eyes and let herself drift into the sensation of the cool breeze and his warm fingers. Forgetting, if only for a moment, how perilous their position still was.

"Come inside," Osiris whispered, dropping his hand to her waist.

Lorna let Osiris guide her into the cave mouth. Once inside, her eyes widened. The walls were painted in elaborate hieroglyphs that shimmered silver in the darkness, almost like they were bio-luminescent. She recognized at once that they were Elven runes; though they were strange and ancient, she couldn't read them.

"Osiris," she whispered, "what is this place?"

Osiris chuckled softly. "I'm not sure. I discovered it years ago when a storm swept through the passes, and I needed shelter. I thought you might like it."

Lorna turned to face him, tears prickling behind her eyes as she murmured, "Osiris Bane, I don't deserve you. I gave you nothing but cold indifference for our whole lives, and you... you..." She choked on her words and could not finish.

Osiris swept to her side and pulled her to him, locking her in his strong arms. He kissed her forehead, then gazed into her eyes and whispered, "Lorna, you deserve the world. And I'm going to give it to you. I'll give you everything I possibly can."

But Lorna knew Osiris could not give her the world. For now, at least, he could only give her the Court of Sky.

And she did not know what waited for her there.

As they sat in the cave gazing out, Osiris's arms tightened around Lorna's waist, and her head came to rest against his chest. The proximity, the weight of his limbs, and the warmth of his body were all strange to her, but as the minutes passed, she relaxed into his embrace.

They watched as the last vestiges of the sun descended behind the distant black peaks of the Funeral Mountains that encircled the place she had once called home. Lorna closed her eyes, a feeling of peace settling over her. Despite the rough stone beneath them, she was comfortable here, cradled by Osiris.

Lorna felt safe here, in this moment, which was more than she had ever felt before. If she never felt it again, at least she had this. The torments of the Shadow Court were behind them, and whatever lay ahead could surely be no worse than what she had survived.

Lorna had nearly dozed off when she felt Osiris's hands moving. His fingers traced along her abdomen, toying with the thin fabric of her robes. Her nipples hardened, puckering as he brushed them lightly with his hands, cupping them, caressing them.

Lorna tilted her head up to look at Osiris's face. He was gazing at her reverently, as if she was the image of the goddess herself, his eyes wide, pupils dilated as he took quick, shallow breaths.

"I want to touch you. All of you." He spoke so softly that Lorna might not have understood his words if she hadn't been watching him and reading his lips.

A trace of a smile crossed her lips. "I want that too. I want you," she whispered, her voice trembling.

Lorna rose, immediately feeling the loss of Osiris's warmth as she unfastened her cloak, letting it fall away, then raised her arms and slipped her robes over her head.

But as she stood there before him, suddenly, she was shy. No man—no one, since her nursemaids as a babe and her sister when she'd whipped her—had ever seen her in the nude before. Shame filled her as she thought about how Osiris had seen her naked, helpless, and pathetic in her sister's throne room. Heat rose in her cheeks, and she clutched the robes to hide her body.

"No," Osiris said forcefully, shaking his head. He got to his feet and approached Lorna, taking her hands. "If you don't want to do this, we won't. But don't be ashamed to show yourself to me."

Lorna trembled, her words dying on the tip of her tongue as she stared at him. She wanted this, had always wanted this. But she couldn't bear to think that he pitied her, that he was doing this because he felt sorry for what she had endured.

Almost as if he had read her mind, Osiris said, "I don't think of you as a broken creature at Ereda's mercy when I see you like this. I've seen fire fae with the wings of a phoenix and sea fae with shimmering scales... but none of them compare to you, Lorna Blackburn. You are the most beautiful creature I've ever laid eyes on. Don't ever hide yourself from me."

Osiris squeezed her hands gently, then released them. And as he stood, immobile as a statue, staring at her, Lorna knew he was speaking the truth.

She choked on a sob and released her grip on the robes, letting them fall to the ground, where they pooled at her feet.

"I want to do this," Lorna breathed and took a step toward Osiris, closing the small distance between them.

With shaking fingers, she removed his cloak and unfastened the buttons of his tunic, revealing his smooth ebon skin, the ridges of his abdominal muscles, the sparse sable hair that covered his chest, the narrow trail of it running down to his Adonis belt.

Tentative, she reached for him, her fingers dancing lightly over his hard musculature. He was not the boy she always relegated him to in her mind. The boy who teased her and tried to make her laugh to no avail. Not anymore. No, Osiris was a man. A gorgeous man. And one who loved her. How had she not seen it sooner? Why had she wasted so many years pushing him away?

Lorna tilted her head up, and when their gazes connected, Osiris's dark eyes burned with desire.

"You're sure?" His voice was husky as he forced the words out past the lump in his throat. "Here? Now? Like this?" Osiris gestured are their surroundings, the hard stone ground of the chilly cave.

Lorna nodded. "Who knows what tomorrow will bring? Tonight, I want to lie with you, Osiris Bane. I want to show you I love you, too."

Standing on tiptoes, Lorna leaned towards Osiris, catching his mouth with hers. This was no kiss like the one he had stolen from her in her chambers. This time, they both gave in completely to their desire.

Their tongues danced, first slow and tentative, then

moving quicker, becoming more desperate to explore and taste.

Osiris's strong hands reached around, grabbing Lorna by the ass and lifting her. She curled her legs around his back, and he carried her to the wall and pressed her up against it, her wings spreading behind her like a shadow moth pinned in place, Osiris the flame she was drawn to.

The stone was rough and cold as it bit into her sensitive, newly healed skin, but she didn't care; the vague discomfort only made the intensity of the pleasure blooming inside her more powerful as he ground his hips against her, his hands squeezing her thighs, his mouth everywhere–her throat, her neck, her lips again.

"I want you inside me," Lorna moaned out between kisses, then bit his neck softly, wanting to mark him, to claim him.

Wordless, Osiris lowered her gently to the floor, laying her body on the soft fabric of his cloak. With shaking hands, he unlaced his breaches and stepped out of them. His manhood stood at attention, as thick and solid as the rest of him, a bead of his essence gleaming on its tip.

Lorna had never been with a man. Her first kiss had been that pilfered moment in her room, which she had brutally shattered with her rebuff. But now... now she felt like she could not live another moment if their bodies didn't come together as one.

"If you're not ready, we can wait. Is this what you want?" Osiris asked again as he towered over her, statuesque in his dark beauty.

But Lorna was tired of his niceties now. She knew what she wanted—no, needed. She didn't just want Osiris. She was so desperate and feverish with her need for him that she couldn't form words. Lorna could only reach out for him, beckoning him to come to her, to enter and join their bodies as one.

Osiris dropped down. He took one of Lorna's nipples in his mouth, swirling his tongue around her areola as he eased into her. He moved slowly, inch by inch until he had filled her, and she gasped as his hips snapped against hers.

Moving rhythmically, he thrust. Stars peppered her vision, and pain, sharp but not unpleasant, pulled a groan from her.

Osiris's lips brushed her ear as he whispered, "I'm not hurting you, am I?"

And he was, but only a little, and the pain mingled with ecstasy and made Lorna feel more alive. She didn't answer except to pull him closer to her, burying his face in her long black tresses. She quickened the pace, her hips rocking, the two moving as one.

The excruciating sensation that her body was on the precipice of something explosive built up, taking her higher and higher until she couldn't hold back anymore.

Her scream shattered the silence of the cave and echoed as she raked her nails down his back and came. Osiris stiffened, and a shudder wracked his body as he found his release, pumping into her.

Then he crashed down, his head finding the curve of her neck, his breath warm on her cheek as they both lay panting in the darkness.

They remained that way for a long time, basking in the warm afterglow, Osiris's arm draped across her abdomen, her fingers tracing patterns on his skin as she stared out into the darkness.

When the rhythm of his breathing steadied, turning slow and deep, and Lorna knew he slept, she closed her eyes and did the same.

A Moment Too Late

Lorna was roused by Osiris murmuring, "Time to wake up, beauty," in her ear.

She didn't want it to be morning...didn't want their night together to end. It had been a beautiful dream, but exposed to the pale pink and gold of the sunrise, that bliss dissipated, replaced by a deep sense of foreboding. Today, they would be on their way, flying out into the cold, crisp mountain air toward a fate unknown.

Lorna stretched and nuzzled Osiris's neck. He took her in his arms, and for a long moment, they lay still, embracing one another. She listened to the steady beating of Osiris's heart, her head resting on his chest, the heat of his body a comfort she didn't want to relinquish. Lorna wished she could remain curled up beside him for hours, days... forever.

Can't we just stay here, hidden away from the rest of the world—my cruel sister and the Shadow Court, whatever new dangers lay in wait in the Court of Sky —forgotten?

But Lorna knew they couldn't.

Remaining here in the borderlands was just as dangerous as staying in the Court of Shadows. Even more dangerous, perhaps, for both the Sky and Shadow courts sent patrols here, ever mistrustful of one another and fearing an incursion into their territory by their rivals.

Osiris kissed her on the forehead, his lips lingering as he swept her hair back behind her ears and said, "We can't stay here," as if he had read her mind.

He was right. Their best chance at escaping Ereda and avoiding being captured by soldiers would be to press on as soon as possible. But something tugged at Lorna, an unnameable sensation that told her if she left this cave, it would be at her peril.

Osiris's words from the previous day came back to her. *It's normal to fear change.* Was that all this was? Not some premonition, but the stress and anxiety of the past few days weighing on her?

Lorna didn't know. But all the same, she stretched and prepared to rise. Her muscles were sore, aching dully from their long flight and passionate lovemaking, but it wasn't unpleasant. The residual pain following the exertion reminded her she was still alive, that come what may, she would be there for it, and Osiris would be by her side.

While Osiris laced his breaches, she pulled her

discarded robes over her head and donned her heavy black cloak. Osiris came up behind her and, with a gentle touch, arranged the folds of fabric around her wings, stroking them.

When Lorna turned around and met his gaze, Osiris asked, "Are you ready?"

Lorna only nodded, afraid the words would catch in her throat if she tried to speak. This was the final leg of their journey. In a few hours, they would reach the Sky Tower. She should be relieved, happy.

So why was she so frightened?

Something dark coiled in her guts, an acrid dread pooling inside her. The rune on her palm pulsed, offering comfort but also a warning. They should not fly. Something terrible was waiting for them out. But how could she explain to Osiris when all she had to go on was a feeling?

He would tell her she was overthinking things—that her restless mind was conjuring up terrors when there was nothing to be afraid of.

So Lorna bit her tongue and said nothing, instead following Osiris out of the cave. Upon emerging into the pale light of pre-dawn, they saw that overnight snow had begun to fall. It whirled in a strong wind that cut Lorna to the bone, making her shudder.

She pulled her cloak tighter around herself for warmth, and Osiris squeezed her arm, smiling at her, but she could see the concern in his eyes, too.

"Is it safe to fly in this weather?" Lorna asked, squinting into the flying flakes.

"I'm sure it's just a squall. Once we get past the peaks

and into the valley, it should settle." Osiris's tone was confident, but his face was drawn, brow furrowed. "Come on," he said, kissing her hand and forcing a smile. "I'll stay close to you. Everything will be fine. I've flown in worse storms than this."

But I haven't, Lorna thought.

And besides, it wasn't the storm itself that frightened her. It was the ominous pall that had fallen over her heart. The feeling that something was deeply, terribly wrong.

Trying to throw it off, she spread her wings and gave Osiris a wan smile.

"Let's be off then. To the Sky Tower. We're almost to our new home."

They took flight, but not with ease.

The wind was a relentless force of nature Lorna had never imagined could exist. It screamed and bellowed like angry shadow fiends as it cut through the gullies, lashing her and Osiris with blinding snow and stinging pellets of ice. Always at their faces as if desperately trying to drive them back whence they'd come.

Even Osiris, accustomed to crossing this border defense, struggled to fly straight and true. For Lorna, who had spent nearly all of her days within the walls of Castle Bleak, just staying aloft was a back-breaking strain. Frozen strands of her hair whipped hair against her face and her lips were blue with the insidious chill that had leached into her bones.

And so their progress was slow. It was difficult to tell time with the sun veiled behind the dense silver cloud cover, but long hours that felt like an eternity passed as

Lorna beat her wings against the raging wind and hammering snow, desperate to make it through the storm.

And then, just as suddenly as it had picked up, the wind died down, the snow becoming pretty, sparkling flurries drifting lazily on the light breeze. Lorna blinked into the sudden stillness, her heart rising, butterflies taking flight in her belly at the sight before them.

Just up ahead, the clouds parted. Sunlight through patches in the clouds, forming haloes on the expanse of the snow-covered valley beneath them.

We made it, Lorna thought, heaving a sigh of relief through lungs that burned from the cold of exertion.

But her breath caught when she turned to Osiris and saw his face twisted into a grimace of horror. She followed his gaze, and her face contorted, too, her hope gutted as her heart shot up into her throat.

For there, streaming through a break in the clouds, were a half dozen Shadow fae warriors, with snapping shadow fiends at their heels, frothing at the mouth. They wore midnight black, with the bat-winged emblem of the Shadow Court proudly displayed on their breasts.

"They aren't allowed to cross the border. Lord Vargas will not tolerate this," Osiris growled.

But whether Ereda had broken a non-aggression pact or not didn't matter. The Shadow fae were here, and Lorna knew who they were after.

Osiris whipped his head around and looked at Lorna.

"Go," he ordered her.

Lorna, too stunned to find words, shook her head

mutely. Go? Where would she go? Onward to the Sky Tower alone? She couldn't, wouldn't. She would never leave Osiris here alone to be taken or, worse, killed.

Osiris gripped Lorna's shoulders roughly, shaking her so hard that her teeth rattled as they knocked together.

"Lorna Blackburn, go! It's you they want, not me. You're the target of your sister's ire. She will kill you if you let them return you to the Court of Shadows. Bleakhart will–" His voice broke on the words, and he could not go on. "Lorna, I swear to you. Ereda will do far worse things to you than she will to me. If you're gone, I can hold them off, perhaps even defeat them. I can't protect you and deal with them at the same time."

Lorna knew it wasn't true. There were too many. Even a skilled and practiced warrior like Osiris, who had defeated dozens of rivals in the Wild Hunt, could not take on so many soldiers with fiends by their sides.

A wail broke from Lorna's throat and hung in the air, eerie and mournful.

Osiris spoke again, his tone gentler but full of urgency. "Please, for me, for the love I bear for you. Go, Lorna. Fly due south and east. The tower isn't far. I promise I will catch up to you. I'll meet you there."

He never would. Lorna knew it was a lie, meant to force her to go. She turned again toward the soldiers, armored from head to toe, rapidly approaching.

Osiris cupped her face in his hands, tilting her gaze back to meet his. He kissed her hard and fast, then whispered, "Please, Lorna, for me. Please go."

Tears streaked her face, freezing as they made contact

with the frigid air. She hitched another sob, then whispered, "I love you, Osiris."

"If you love me, then go."

She could not stand the heartbreak in his eyes, and she knew he was right. If she stayed, she would die on this day.

And so, though her heart fought the motion with everything in it, Lorna turned away from Osiris, pumped her wings, and flew, heading southeast for the Tower of Sky.

Alone.

Court of Sky

The air warmed as Lorna moved south, but she did not feel it, for she was frozen inside. The frigid tears on her cheeks melted, but her heart felt encased in ice. If she let her emotions thaw, she could not go on. She would disintegrate, evaporate, fade into nothing if she stopped to think about Osiris, the Shadow fae soldiers, and what had just happened. The hole she felt inside herself would become all-consuming. Her pain and grief would devour, and there would be nothing left.

Lorna was sure of it.

So instead, she flew as fast as her weary, strained wings could carry her. Not because she feared her sister or cared about her own life. Not even because she had vowed to Osiris that she would. But because Lorna did not know what else to do. She wasn't afraid she would get caught, but she was terrified of simply falling apart. Of disappearing into the black abyss of pain forever.

If any of the Shadow Fae stalked her on her long journey, Lorna did not see them. In fact, she saw almost nothing. Her tears blinded her eyes. Her broken soul processed nothing but pain; her surroundings were just a blur passing by.

She had lost him. Probably forever. Osiris was gone, sent to Bleakhart to be tortured, possibly killed, and it was all her fault.

So she flew. On and on. Perhaps she would never stop. She would just go on forever until her wings gave out. And then whatever happened from there would be what it was. She didn't even know how far she had traveled or for how long she had flown when it suddenly appeared.

The Sky Tower.

A single, gleaming white pinnacle slashed the horizon, higher than any cloud bank had ever dreamt of drifting. Below, the castle proper looked to be chiseled from ivory, with an abundance of smaller towers and courtyards scattered at a base embraced by swirling white vapor. Lorna could see when she looked closer that the structure had been carved into the pale pink quartz of the mountains on its western side. But the whole palace seemed to be floating at a glance—a castle in the sky.

Lorna would have flown right by in her daze of heartache and misery if it had been less majestic and awe-inspiring. But even in her shattered state, the sight of the Sky Tower brought her to a halt as her eyes widened, and she took it in.

The rune on her palm pulsed in reassurance, sending heat through her, and as she gazed up at this strange, magical sight in this foreign land, Lorna made a decision.

She might never be happy again. She was certain she wouldn't. But as long as she was alive, she would honor Osiris and the elves and follow her fate. She would live the prophecy Muírgan Vivane had seen in the stars and ally with anyone who would stand against the Shadow Empress and the wanton death and destruction she would bring to the Ethereal Realms.

Lorna took a shaky breath and resumed her course to the Sky fae seat of power. Her wings burned so intensely with each stroke that when, moments later, a voice shouted, "Halt!" she was almost relieved.

Dropping to the pale silvery earth gracelessly, Lorna crash-landed on her knees. The voice had come from above, and when she tilted her head up, she got her first glimpse of a Sky fae.

She was surprised to see it was a woman, clad all in pale blue and white, her silver-blonde hair pulled back in an elaborate but severe braided twist. She wore a thin silver rapier at her hip, and the air around her swirled in a menacing maelstrom.

The Sky fae landed beside Lorna, planting her feet in the dirt. The air magic still eddied around her.

She narrowed her eyes in suspicion as she spoke. "Shadow fae are forbidden from crossing the blizzard border into Sky." Her voice was matter-of-fact, and she planted her hands on her hips as she glowered down at the woman she assumed was an intruder.

Lorna fought to catch her breath, her weariness

taking hold of her all at once. White spots danced in her vision, but she forced herself to remain on her knees.

She couldn't raise her head to meet the woman's gaze, but she choked out, "I am aware. But I come at the invitation of Lord Vargus."

The Sky fae let out a short burst of laughter and, for a moment, looked as if she would accuse Lorna of lying. Then her eyes widened, and her hand came up to cover her mouth.

When she let it drop again, having mastered her surprise, the Sky fae whispered, "You... You are the Shadow's Sister."

A spark of fury Lorna didn't think she had in her kindled white and hot as she looked up, meeting startled ice-blue eyes.

"Not anymore," Lorna Blackburn replied.

"We need to get you inside the tower. It isn't safe for you out here." The Sky fae woman's words came out in a rush, and her expression darkened as she went on, "Not all my brethren will be pleased to know we've taken a Shadow fae into the fold. They even found fault with Osiris when he—"

She halted, her crystal blue eyes narrowing and scanning their surroundings, flitting across silver-grassed fields around them, over the distant snow-capped peaks, then up to the cloud-banded sky.

She looked back at Lorna and asked, "Where is Osiris? I understood he was to escort you." Her tone changed, becoming sad and soft as if she'd already put two and two together but hoped she was wrong.

Hearing her lost love's name sucked Lorna's breath

away as surely as a swift kick to the gut, and she couldn't answer except with a shake her head.

But that was all that was needed.

The Sky fae grimaced, and Lorna was surprised to see she looked genuinely distraught. Osiris must have been telling the truth when he said he'd grown close with many in the Court of Sky.

"That is not good news. My people have found a surprising ally in the emissary. Just as we hope to with you." The look she gave Lorna was pointed. Was it a thinly veiled threat? Lorna couldn't be sure. She was too weary and distraught to determine the intention behind the Sky fae's words. The silver-haired woman sighed, then continued, "Perhaps my father can secure his release," the Sky fae offered.

"Your father?" Lorna echoed dully.

Who was this woman? More importantly, who was her father? Lorna should be able to piece it together on her own, but it was difficult to think. Her mind felt muddled, her thoughts disjointed, and stringing ideas together to make connections felt impossible. Clearly, this Sky fae knew Osiris, and she must be well-connected if she thought her father could help him escape Ereda's. No mere palace guard, then.

A smile tugged at the warrior woman's lips, the first Lorna had seen, illuminating her, changing her cold countenance to something beautiful and shining. Then it passed as quickly as it had come as she explained, "I'm Violetta Skyborn, daughter of Lord Vargas and the late Lady Svetlana. Heir to the Court of Sky."

Lorna blinked, surprised that a woman of such high

status - the heir apparent - should be clad in armor and seemingly on patrol. Ereda always spoke of how weak and pathetic the Sky Fae were. That was not the impression Violetta gave off by any far stretch of the imagination.

She knew she should curtsy in the presence of the heir to the Sky Court, but she was too unsteady to manage it. Instead, Lorna dipped her head, hoping that would be sufficient respect.

Violetta seemed not at all interested in the formality. Instead, she reached down, took Lorna's hands in a strong, firm grip, and helped her to her feet.

"Come, Lorna," she said, her tone brusque and all business but not unkind. "We have much to discuss, but not out here. And my father will be longing to see you."

Lorna shuddered at the idea of walking into that throne room without Osiris by her side. The palace looming before them was beautiful beyond imagining, but there was also something cold about it. Truth be told, she felt the same way about Violetta, with her pristine silvery beauty and her alert, penetrating gaze.

"I know you must be weary from your journey, but can you fly a bit more? Just on to the tower? I can call the wind to help you on your way." Violetta cocked her head at Lorna.

The rune sent off a pulse in Lorna's palm. This was her destiny. She'd come this far; she would take the next step.

Lorna nodded and stretched her wings, the burning muscles screaming in protest as they opened wide. But the pain was nothing compared to the ache of longing in her heart.

"Good," Violetta said with a nod.

Then, without another word, the Sky fae took flight, her white dove's wings carrying her towards the Sky Tower.

Lorna set off behind her. The magic tailwind Violetta had conjured did most of the work, ushering her towards whatever uncertain future awaited in the white marble confines she moved rapidly towards.

Second Sons and Daughters

The Sky Tower was no less dazzling inside than out and as different from Castle Bleak as night and day. Lorna marveled at the elaborate tapestries depicting pegasus, unicorns, and more ethereal white-winged beings like Violetta, woven in shimmering white and cloth-of-gold with silver borders bedecking every wall. The floor was marbled blue and gold, gleaming beneath the Starbursts of blue faerie fire torches.

She limped behind Violetta, struggling to keep pace with the Sky fae as she led the way down a long hallway to a foyer from which a curved staircase led to the tower's uppermost levels.

They bypassed the steps, skirting around them to another corridor, which twisted downward. And, while markedly different from the dismal black tunnels that led to the Undercity in the Shadow Court, the trajectory still caused a hitch in Lorna's step.

Was she being led to the dungeons?

With the thought, Lorna broke out in a cold sweat and became light-headed. She staggered, leaning against the wall for support, fighting for her breath as her heart thundered in her ears. The soft fabric of a tapestry brushed her cheek, and she turned to press her forehead against it, willing her head to clear.

Violetta's footsteps ground to a halt. She turned around and made her way back to where Lorna stood. In her peripheral vision, Lorna saw her pale blue eyes assessing her coolly.

Then she cocked her head and asked, "Is something the matter?" There was no warmth in her tone nor anger. If anything, the Sky fae sounded matter-of-fact and a bit concerned.

Lorna swallowed hard and struggled to master her breathing. Violetta's eyes didn't move, her aquamarine gaze intent and perhaps curious.

Finally, Lorna found the words. "Are you bringing me to the dungeon?" she asked with a quivering voice.

A hint of that radiance Lorna had seen earlier when Violetta smiled crossed her face again as the Sky fae tried to smother a laugh with a serious expression.

Her iciness thawed a bit more as she placed a hand gently on Lorna's shoulder and said. "I have heard the Court of Shadows is a... difficult place. And that the empress is a cruel master to serve. We are not like that in the Sky Court. We're going to the throne room, where you'll meet my father, who I'm sure you'll find a measured, reasonable man."

A smile flickered on Violetta's face again, brightening it. "And besides, we don't have dungeons. Our prison cells are in a tower. If I planned to lock you away for the crime of being born who you are, we'd be going up, not down." Violetta gave Lorna a much-appreciated moment to gather herself, then said, "You've nothing to worry about. All right now?"

The relief that passed through Lorna wasn't so much a wave as a trickle, but it was enough that she managed a slight nod to Violetta. She pushed off the wall again and resumed following the Sky fae, who slowed her stride considerably now in a thoughtful gesture, giving Lorna time to get her bearings.

After a few more minutes of heading down, the corridor leveled and widened. Here, large windows comprised both walls, revealing a breathtaking view of the white-capped mountains that hemmed in the Sky Tower on two sides.

It would have been beautiful if seeing those peaks didn't stir the sordid memories of what had happened to Osiris on their journey over them in Lorna. Tears pricked behind her eyes, but she forced them back as they approached huge double doors flanked by Sky fae guards in pale blue and silver armor, similar to Violetta's but less ornate.

It wasn't the time to cry. Lorna could weep to her heart's content later. Now, she had to meet the Skylord. And she'd need her wits about her as best as she could manage.

Violetta nodded to one of the guards, who opened the door, stepped into the throne room, and announced, "The Lady Violetta."

Beckoning Lorna, Violetta stepped inside.

Lorna followed...

And stared at the most stunningly gorgeous man she'd ever seen.

He lounged on the throne with one leg crossed over the other. His build was so slender, he might have been effeminate, were his lithe muscles not so well defined, and if his very demeanor didn't radiate almost toxic masculinity. Hair so pale it could only be described as moonlight-hued framed a striking, though currently sullen, alabaster-skinned face, his eyes the same cool blue hue as Violetta's but flecked with tiny bits of silver.

Unsure what the customs were in the Court of Sky, Lorna dropped into a low curtsy and murmured, "My Lord."

She heard a snort beside her and looked up, surprised to see Violetta scowling at the man seated on the throne.

"No need to bow to my brother," she said, taking Lorna's elbow and guiding her back up from her curtsy.

Her brother?

Lorna's cheeks heated with shame. She should have known. This man—just a boy, really, now that she looked closer—could not possibly be the great and powerful Vargas Skyborn.

"Get off the throne, Varik," Violetta chided her brother with an exasperated sigh.

Varik smirked but did as he was asked, giving Violetta

an exaggerated bow as he hopped gracefully down from the dais and stretched his wings.

If Violetta's downy, white-feathered wings were beautiful, Varik's were even more so, with shots of silver and gold forming elaborate patterns. Lorna clenched her hands into fists as she was struck with the bizarre and inappropriate urge to touch them, to feel how soft they were.

"Where's Father?" Violetta demanded, her tone all business, making it clear she didn't have time for her brother's chicanery.

Varik shrugged, the gesture lazy and feline. "I don't know. He had me summoned. To yell at me about something I've done wrong, I'm sure." His radiant eyes rolled heavenward, and his smirk deepened.

Violetta let out perhaps the world-weariest sigh Lorna had ever heard, then snapped, "Both of you stay here. I'm going to get Father. Varik, don't even speak to her while I'm gone. Just stand there and don't talk." She looked at Lorna, her tone softening, and said, "Ignore my brother and anything he might say to you. He has no manners and makes an ass out of himself. I'll be back with the Skylord."

Violetta turned and stormed from the room, her boots clicking on the blue marble floor.

Lorna bunched the fabric of her cloak in her fist, twisting it nervously between her fingers, eyes trained on the ground.

Varik, apparently having no intention of heeding his sister's order, waited only until he heard the click of the door behind, indicating Violetta was out of earshot, before drawling, "So you're the mysterious Shadow's Sister."

He walked around Lorna in a slow circle, which made her intensely uncomfortable. She felt like livestock under his scrutiny and was surprised he didn't yank her lips back to examine her teeth as the stablemen did with Night Mares and Unicorns.

The name rankled, but she didn't correct him, only acquiesced, "I am Lorna Blackburn, sister of Ereda Blackburn, the Shadow empress," not giving him the gratification of repeating the loathed nickname.

"Ah, so you don't appreciate being compared to your older, better half, either." The words weren't kind, but there was no malice in his tone. And when Lorna looked up, Varik wore a playful smile.

Annoyed, Lorna crossed her arms and said, "She's only older by a moment."

Varik's brows lifted at this, and he tilted his head to one side. "And is she better?" he pressed.

Lorna frowned, uncertain. "I suppose that depends on what you mean by better," she answered with a shrug.

Varik chuckled and arched a brow. "Between the sheets, I mean. You're far prettier than her. I saw your sister once before when my mother brought me to the Wild Hunt. But I've had pretty girls before who were about as skilled at lovemaking as a dead fish."

Heat rose in Lorna's cheeks. Her first instinct was to hurl a shadow bolt at him and teach him some of the manners his sister correctly surmised he was lacking and mar that perfect, milky skin of his. But given that he was the son of the Skylord, that would not be an appropriate response. She clenched her fists again to conceal the gray smoke simmering on her fingertips.

If Varik noticed the shadows coalescing around Lorna, he didn't pay them any mind. He only gave her a roguish smile and declared, "I'll tell you a secret."

As he stepped closer to her, the scent of wind and rain nearly overwhelmed Lorna. She felt light-headed and giddy as he leaned in, pressed his lips to her ear, and whispered, "I don't like being compared to my sister."

Lorna stiffened as he backed off a step and grinned, then dipped into a low bow, his cloak swirling around him. He looked up at her through a fringe of silver lashes and winked.

"It's a pleasure to meet you, Lorna Blackburn. What a fine pair we are. Two second-born children who killed our mothers coming out of the womb, neither of us much more than a pawn to do our family's bidding. Perhaps our fathers will propose a union between us, hmm? Uniting Sky and Shadow under the eyes of the Goddess."

Varik snorted out a burst of laughter, and Lorna almost choked on air as she tried to stifle her surprised gasp. What was she to say without insulting this rude, obnoxious boy and getting herself locked up in the tower for it?

"We do not honor consorts as Lords in the Court of Shadows, so I never knew my father," she murmured.

Varik gave her a disarming grin and said, "Well then, I guess it's up to the esteemed Lord Vargas what to do with us then. A pinnacle of honor and virtue without an interesting bone in his body. I doubt if he's creative enough to—"

The door to the throne room was flung open, and Varik backed away from Lorna as the guard announced, "Lord Vargas and Violetta Skyborn."

When Lord Vargas strode into the room with Violetta on his heels, not even pausing to acknowledge Lorna or his son, Lorna wondered how she could possibly have mistaken Varik for him.

The Skylord was not dissimilar in appearance from his offspring, with the same keen blue eyes and silvery blond hair, though unlike Violetta with her braids and Varik with his long, loose style, Vargas wore his trimmed to just above the ears with a well-groomed beard dusting his chin.

It was the Skylord's bearing that truly set him apart, though. He carried himself in much the same way as Lorna's sister, with an unquestionable air of authority in his every glance and motion as he perched upon his throne and lifted a silver diadem from a cushioned table, setting it on his brow.

Lorna's palms sweated. She knew nothing of this man, and now her entire destiny lay in his hands. But her rune pulsed, sending a wave of reassurance through her, helping her keep her breathing in check.

She would not melt down here.

"Lorna Blackburn, I presume?" Lord Vargas inquired in a surprisingly soft-spoken voice, fixing her with an unreadable look.

"Yes, My Lord," Lorna answered.

She dipped into a low curtsy and held it until the Skylord said, "You may rise, child."

Upon rising and straightening, Lorna felt everyone's eyes on her - Lord Vargas, Violetta, and Varik - and the sensation made her skin crawl.

After a beat of silence, Vargas began with, "We have much to discuss, Lady Blackburn. But first..." He dropped off and turned to face Varik, skewering his son with an angry glare that made Lorna flinch on his behalf. "I had hoped to speak to you in private. But since it took you *four hours,"*—his tone sharpened further—"to heed my summons, now your sister and our guest can hear of your shame as well. Hopefully, the embarrassment will serve as a reminder to behave like the prince you are, not some wayward scoundrel. What if something had happened, and I needed your urgent assistance, Varik?"

Lorna looked at Varik, noting that he did not appear chastened in the slightest. His hands were on his narrow hips, his lips set in a haughty smirk. She could not imagine responding to Ereda's beratement with such... what was the word for it? Audacity? Arrogance? She didn't even know. Responding in such a way to her sister was so far outside the realm of possibility, she wasn't even sure there was a word for it.

Varik didn't answer his father's question, only sighed, tossing his pale hair, and toeing the floor, looking bored.

"I was here before you," he said with a shrug.

"I waited three hours and didn't see hide nor hair of you. And you waltz after the fourth hour and now imply *I* am the one who was late?" Vargas boomed, his voice loud as the thunder of his magic harnessed.

Lorna shuddered at the sound, though Varik seemed completely unphased. She had unconsciously taken two steps back, away from the throne, when Violetta put a hand on her shoulder and smiled reassuringly.

"Don't worry. Father only gets like this with Varik. Because he's a spoiled, selfish, insufferable brat. He won't shout at you."

In fact, Vargas's voice had already dropped to a soft, calm, but deadly serious drone as he said, "If I catch you or hear so much as a whispered rumor about you whoring all over Sky and throwing faerie-wine-fueled orgies–"

Lorna blushed at Vargas' accusations, then gasped as Varik cut his father off. Ereda would have had her head in a heartbeat for this response.

"Well, there will always be rumors, father. I reputation to uphold–"

"No more rumors. No more parties. No more rutting with concubines or staying out until the first light. It ends today!" Vargas bellowed, the faintest tinge of red lighting his frosty white cheeks as he pounded his fist on the throne so hard the room around them seemed to tremble.

Then his voice dropped an octave again, deep, low, and severe. "No more chances for you, Varik. From now on, your half-brother is your bodyguard. Braedin will be with you everywhere you go and in everything you do to ensure your behavior is appropriate for a prince of Sky."

Lorna noticed that with this, Varik's look of minor irritation had faltered, his expression now resembling something more like utter horror.

"I'm not a child to be followed around by a babysitter!" Varik burst out. His blue eyes smoldered, and a breeze had begun to swirl around him, blowing his hair back from his face.

"Until you can act like an adult—and more importantly, a prince—that is the way of it. Now get out of my sight."

Varik narrowed his eyes as if he would protest further, but in the end, he only shot his father a hateful glare, then turned on his heel and stalked towards the throne room exit. Lorna was sure she heard a muffled snicker from Violetta beside her as he went.

"Go with him. See that he behaves himself." Vargas turned his head.

A figure Lorna had not even realized was present, with long, gracefully curved antlers, mahogany hair, and white wings speckled with gold and red spots, stepped from behind the throne, bowed his head, and briskly followed Varik out the door.

The half-brother, she guessed, though the two bore little resemblance beyond their feathered wings.

Glancing down, Lorna noticed the water on her skin, the storm of the Sky prince's emotions having been enough to conjure rain.

"And you," Vargas spoke again, directing his gaze at Lorna.

She stiffened and looked up, expecting some rebuke or interrogation, but all Vargas said was, "I'm sorry you had to see that. You must be wondering how a man can rule an entire court but be unable to master his own son."

Lorna stood like a deer in headlights, unsure how to

answer. The Skylord didn't look angry; to the contrary, he just looked sad and weary, as if a great weight rested on his shoulder, almost too heavy to bear. He looked like an entirely different man from the poised, confident ruler who had strode into the throne room not long before. She twisted her damp, dirty robes nervously, but she was saved from having to respond by Violetta.

She gave her father a sympathetic look and consoled, with a gentle voice, "Varik was born wild. He's as untamed as a storm blowing in over the mountains. We've all tried to rein him in, father. It isn't your fault he is the way he is. Perhaps Braedin will have better luck. They have always been close, and he will be a good influence."

"The boy needed a mother's calming touch. It was cruel of the Goddess to take her from him. And you too, Violetta. But Varik... I could never strongarm him into submission; all it did was drive him away. Perhaps if I had met Cozette sooner..."

Who is Cozette? Lorna wondered, then silently chastised herself for her nosiness. The conversation was actually uncomfortable to overhear. Lorna had no right to eavesdrop on the Skyborn family's inner turmoil. But the mention of Varik's mother struck a chord in her, for she knew entirely too well what it was like to live a life bereft of a mother's care.

Of course, she did not say that. It wasn't her place. She only waited in silence, staring at the swirling blue and gray marble patterns on the floor, until Vargas sighed deeply and finally resumed.

"But past mistakes must be left to lie. And you have

come a long way, Lady Blackburn, and not to hear about the trial of fathering a wayward son. Tell me, where is Osiris?"

Lorna's musings on the loss of her mother vanished, replaced by a pang of fresher, newer loss, which hit her so hard she almost doubled over as the wave of grief broke over her. She could not find the words to tell the Skylord what had happened to her lover as tears pooled anew, sliding down her cheeks unchecked.

Again, Violetta came to her aid. "It seems Osiris did not complete the journey. It's plainly difficult for Lady Blackburn to speak on the matter. The poor thing is traumatized. But my understanding is that they were waylaid by Ereda's forces, and the lady was able to escape, but Osiris Bane was not."

Lorna's thoughts pivoted away from Osiris to Violetta's words, seeking any distraction from her pain. Why did everyone keep calling her 'Lady'? Her sister was the lady, the empress of the Shadow Court. Was this some strange custom of the Sky Fae to call all those related to royalty lord and lady?

"I see," Lord Vargas murmured, then he went on, his voice hardening a touch. "Lady Blackburn, I do not wish to distress you further, but we must come to an understanding about your tenure here. Then, I will let you recover from what I'm sure was a harrowing journey."

Lorna wiped her eyes with the backs of her hands and nodded to the Skylord.

Her voice quavered as she said, "Of course, my Lord. I am your humble servant. Whatever you ask of me, I shall do." Silently, she added, *For it cannot be worse than what my sister has asked of me.*

Vargas drummed his fingers on the arm of his throne, studying Lorna, then nodded slowly.

"War is coming," he said, and his tight tone made it clear he took no joy in this fact. "I do not know what alliances will be made or where the chips will fall. I only know that your sister, the Shadow Empress, will likely be our enemy. Understand this is not something I want—war or enemies. I had hoped we might avoid such an end, but..." Vargas sighed and dropped off.

Lorna was grave as she said, "My sister is doing unspeakable things with terrible, ancient magic, long forgotten but rediscovered by her sorcerer. If there's any path that avoids open war with her, you should take it." Hoping Vargas would not take the comment the wrong way, she added, "I am sure your soldiers are brave and strong, but the things my sister—"

The Skylord raised a hand, giving her a stern look, and Lorna closed her mouth, biting off her words.

"I am aware of the goings on within the dungeons of Castle Bleak and your sister's sorcerer. I have eyes and ears within the Shadow Court to keep me abreast of the situation. Or I did until very recently."

Vargas gave Lorna a pointed look, and she suddenly realized—*He means Osiris!*

The thought gave her pause. How long had Osiris been working both sides, in the confidence of her sister and the Skylord? Osiris had told her he had ties in the Sky Court, but she hadn't realized what a dangerous game he'd been playing. If either Ereda or Vargas had any suspicion, he was feeding their secrets to the other side...

She shuddered to think of the consequences.

Vargas seemed to notice she'd been driven to distraction and cleared his throat.

With an inward wince, Lorna bowed her head. "Apologies, my Lord. So much has happened so quickly. I find myself..." She dropped off, unsure how much to say.

Certainly, she would not inform him that Osiris had been playing both sides of the same coin all this time. That would be to betray him—or his memory, if that was all that was left of him. Would Ereda have him killed? She did not know.

But the more pressing question was: was it now her *duty* to betray the man she loved?

When Vargas spoke, he might have picked the words right out of Lorna's mind.

"Osiris Bane was always a bit of a wild card, truth be told. Impossible to know where his loyalties lay, in truth. I did not grow to be so old and wise,"—he chuckled as he spoke the last word, as if he wasn't really sure it was true—"by being a fool, Lady Blackburn."

His icy blue eyes burned into Lorna's, his gaze so penetrating she felt sure the Skylord could see the very contents of her soul. She shivered under the intensity of his gaze.

Then he went on. "But what of you, Lady Lorna Blackburn? You may loathe Ereda's machinations, but she is still your sister. Surely you have some love and loyalty left for her in your heart?"

Lorna did not pause to measure her response, and when she spoke, her words were full of venom. "My sister is as much my enemy as she is yours. No loyalty to her remains. I have no family, save Ereda, and no friends in Shadow Court. I was ignored by most, reviled and tormented by a few for being different. I can say, in all honesty, I have no love for anyone in my court, my Lord."

But it was a lie. For unless he was dead, Osiris was still in the Shadow Court.

And Osiris was the one person in the world Lorna could claim to have ever loved, though the love was fledgling and new.

A slow smile crossed the Skylord's lips, and he said, "This is as I hoped. And all I will ask of you is all the Shadow Empress's secrets spilled to me and your help to destroy her. That is the cost of Sanctuary here. And perhaps, one day, the prize will be an empire of your own."

Lorna's heart thudded in alarm. An empire of her own? If she hadn't known Lord Vargas had every intention of deposing Ereda, it was clear as day now.

Lorna should feel some sorrow or guilt at the idea of killing her only living relative, but all she felt was a creeping dread. What made the Skylord think he could defeat the most powerful fae court in the Ethereal Realms? And even if the Sky fae were, by some miracle, victorious in that crusade... Lorna had no desire to rule over anything or anyone save herself. She would not trade the yoke of Ereda's demands for the concerns of an entire kingdom.

She wasn't born for it. Wasn't built for it.

And she almost said so, but the rune on her palm pulsed as if with a warning. A time would come to speak of such misgivings but now was not it.

Lorna nodded and forced a smile she was sure more closely resembled a grimace. Bowing her head in acquiescence, she said, "I will help in any way that I can, My Lord. Any knowledge or secrets I am privy to are as good as yours."

The severe expression faded from the Skylord's face, replaced with a genuine smile that illuminated his countenance much the way Violetta's did.

"That's wonderful news," Vargas declared, then turned his gaze to Violetta. "Will you show Lady Blackburn to her quarters, daughter? The empty rooms near Cozette's."

Again, the stranger's name was mentioned, and whoever this Cozette was, a fondness came into the Skylord's tone when he spoke of her. A sibling, perhaps? Another daughter? Lorna suddenly wished that in all the reading she'd done in her life, she had paid even a sliver as much attention to the great fae families as to Elven lineage.

If she had, she might not feel so confused and overwhelmed now.

"Come," Violetta said in what Lorna was coming to know as her usual cursory tone.

"Thank you again, My Lord. You have saved me from certain death, and come what may, I will do my best to repay the debt," Lorna said, hoping she sounded sincere.

In truth, she was concerned. She had escaped Ereda's

plots but now felt she had been thrown into a whole new world of intrigue and schemes, alone, in an unfamiliar place, surrounded by strangers with no idea if she could trust them. Would Vargas be so keen to have her around once she'd given him all she knew about her sister and his plans? Was the comment about her empire only bait for a carefully set trap?

All this ran through Lorna's head as she followed Violetta through the winding, mazelike corridors that comprised the lower levels of the Sky Tower, struggling to keep up with her long strides and quick pace.

Finally, Violetta stopped in front of one of several doors lining the hallway, opened it, and gestured for Lorna to step inside.

Lorna wasn't sure what she'd been expecting. Something more like her quarters in the Shadow Court, perhaps. Small, simple, serviceable. Or perhaps a dungeon cell.

Whatever she'd anticipated, this room was anything but. The space yawned out from the doors, vast and ornately furnished with a huge four-poster bed draped in lavish blue and white linens, several dressers, and a white elm rolltop desk. Double doors opened to a veranda with gauzy white curtains pulled open to reveal a stunning view of the courtyards below and the distant mountains.

But that wasn't what took Lorna's breath away. To her utter amazement, a vast bookshelf spanned the length of the entire wall opposite the bed, filled with tomes and scrolls.

All the doubts and misgivings Lorna had about the Sky Court were put aside, at least for the moment. As if hypnotized, Lorna crossed the room. Her fingers traced over the stones and fragile rolled parchment. Her eyes flitted wildly to take it all in: histories, anatomy books, spell books, Elven lore.

"How did you know to do this?" Lorna whispered, looking back at Violetta, who lingered in the doorway.

A wistful look crossed the Sky fae's moon-pale face. "Osiris told us you have a love for the written word and are a skilled translator."

Osiris. Of course. The only person in the world who knew her—her likes and dislikes, her passions. Or at least, the only person who cared enough to take them into account.

Lorna wanted to cry, but the well of her tears had seemingly run dry. She didn't even feel sorrow anymore, only hollow, empty, and desperately alone.

"I appreciate your thoughtfulness more than you can know." At least with the library right here in her room, she would have an escape. "Please tell the Skylord that," she said earnestly.

One of Violetta's rare, radiant smiles appeared. "You are most welcome. But I'm sure you are beyond weary. The water room is right there if you want to wash away the dust of your journey." She pointed to the door across from the bed. "You'll find some... more appropriate attire,"—with this, her eyes raked up and down Lorna, and she wrinkled her nose—"in the closet."

Lorna nodded numbly but didn't say a word. She couldn't. The weight of everything that had happened hung over her like a guillotine blade waiting to drop as she stood in the huge, elegant room with this stranger. Soon it would overwhelm her. She had nothing left.

Seeming to recognize this, Violetta gave her a cursory nod and said, "I'll have food sent up. Rest now. We'll speak more once you've had some time to gather yourself.

And with that, the Sky fae left the room, closing the door with a quiet click.

The Reckoning

Alone, Lorna crumbled. She never made it to the water room to take the bath she so desperately needed and didn't even bother to remove her damp, soiled garments. She simply slipped the cloak from her shoulders, let it fall to the floor, and then climbed into bed.

The sheets were silky, with a thick, soft feather bed beneath them that felt like lying on a cloud. But all the comfort did was remind Lorna that while she was here, safe—at least for the moment—Osiris was in her sister's clutches.

Had she locked him in one of the Undercity's cold, dank, dismal prison cells? Even now, was Bleakhart torturing him to find out where Lorna had gone and how Ereda might get her back and make her pay for defecting to the enemies?

Lorna tried to remember how long it had been since Bleakhart had made the terrible demand of her that drove her to defy her sister. It felt like ages had passed since she'd stood in that chamber full of malevolence and watched the old sorcerer perform the most hideous blood magic—necromancy.

Lorna shuddered, remembering the mindless, sightless eyes of the reanimated elf. Bleakhart hadn't mastered the spell yet, but she knew, even without her, he eventually would. All her departure had done was buy time.

She hoped Vargas had a brilliant plan in mind to defeat Ereda because even without the addition of the undead in her army, the Shadow Court ranks were mighty and formidable. Whatever Osiris had told the Skylord, she didn't think Vargas understood the full breadth and scope of Ereda's army and the terror her sister would rain down on the Sky Court if it came to open war.

Lorna closed her eyes, her heart aching dully in her chest, desperate not to think of these things anymore. Her weariness was so great that she slipped into a deep slumber the moment her vision went dark.

But as Lorna slept, she dreamed.

Where was she? Somewhere she had never been before. The air shimmered faintly, as if stardust were caught in it, glittering with specks of pink and gold. Titanous trees with broad, cupped leaves of green and gold towered overhead,

and in the distance, a shining city on a hill. Tall, slender towers sparkled like massive prisms as they reflected the bright light, throwing back rainbows.

The City of Glass—the stronghold of the strange, elusive dreamers and the last sanctuary of the elves. It had to be. Lorna had never seen it before, but she'd read countless descriptions. Nowhere else in the Realms resembled the famed city of scholars, artists, and fae with mysterious powers to control the mind.

She found herself moving toward the city without even realizing she was moving. Not walking or flying, but being propelled toward it in that way dreams have of carrying you to distant places. Around her, the sky changed from day to night, stars appearing one by one to puncture the black velvet of the heavens. Lorna marveled at how much brighter they seemed here.

When she stopped, she stood at the gates. A group gathered in the circular courtyard just beyond the high, glittering walls. Elves and Dreamers stood side by side in an ellipse, all dressed in flowing, white robes. In the center of the semi-circle they formed, the air wavered and sparked, blue lightning bolts streaking down and sizzling as they hit the scorched earth.

Watching, a sudden deep sense of dread and foreboding fell over her like a pall.

What are they doing? *Lorna wondered. Clearly some sort of spell but—*

Before she could muse more on the nature of the magic, something in the air changed. The pressure plunged, causing her ears to pop and her nose to run. When she brought her fingers to it, they came away red with blood.

A tremendous crash sounded, and Lorna screamed in agony as her eardrums shattered. Then a flash of brilliant white light—leaving her spinning, blind into an abyss of whiteness. She screamed, but it was soundless, swallowed up by the tremendous roar of the continued explosions.

Lorna awoke with a start, drenched in sweat, tangled in the sheets. Her heart thumped frantically, blood thrumming through her veins, and the rune on her palm seared like a firebrand.

She blinked rapidly, relieved to find that at least she wasn't blinded for life as her eyes adjusted to the darkness around her. Only the pale light of the twin crescent moons streaming through the open curtains of the balcony illuminated the unfamiliar chamber.

The Sky Court. Lorna remembered now. She was safe and in the Court of Sky.

It was only a dream. A nightmare, brought on by all the stress of recent events, she told herself.

But the rune on her palm pulsed, hot and painful in warning.

Not a dream.

A message from Fate. A sliver of destiny.

Lorna was still catching her breath and trying to slow her racing heart when she heard the soft knock on her chamber door. She wiped her face with her hands, brushed her tangled hair out of her eyes, and rubbed away the still-wet tears. She noted with some dismay that her robes smelled musty and were still damp.

The knock sounded again.

She hesitated a moment, then climbed out of bed and padded to the door, cracking it open.

A strawberry-haired woman stood in the doorway, butterfly wings swirled with tangerine and gold held aloft behind her. Her pale brow furrowed with concern as her golden eyes surveyed Lorna.

She blinked once to make sure she wasn't still dreaming. She wasn't. The woman, who was certainly a Dreamer, remained standing in the doorway when she opened her eyes.

But who was she, and why was she here?

They just stared at one another for a moment until the woman asked in a soft, melodic voice, "Is everything all right?"

Lorna peered at her, confused. Everything most certainly was not all right in the grand scheme of things. But what had brought her to Lorna's door right now?

"Everything is fine. Why do you ask?" Lorna choked out from her parched throat. When was the last time she'd eaten or drunk anything? She couldn't recall.

The Dreamer smiled faintly and said, "I'm Cozette. Lord Vargas's mistress. My rooms are next to yours, and as I lay in bed, I sensed... strife. Mental... screaming." She blushed, her freckled cheeks pinking. "It's an unusual ability, I know. I did not mean to intrude. I just feared something might be amiss."

Ah, that, Lorna thought.

This was why most of the other fae feared the

Dreamers—including Ereda. They were solitary and generally peaceful folk, who preferred studying astrology and history above waging war, but their powers were strange and ill-understood.

It was said the Dreamers could get inside your mind and pluck thoughts from it. Or even plant false memories or drive a person to the brink of madness with wild delusions.

But looking at Cozette, Lorna didn't see a threat. She saw a kindred spirit, for the Skylord's mistress, like herself, was a long way from home, surrounded by people who were not her own.

Lorna opened to door a little wider and gave Cozette a weak smile. "A dream," she said. "It was only a dream." Though she knew that was a lie. "I'm Lorna Blackburn, newly arrived from the Court of Shadows," she introduced herself to change the topic.

Whether Cozette knew she was the Shadow Empress's sister and simply didn't care or not, Lorna wasn't sure. But she didn't seem concerned or put off by the admission—a surprise since the rancor between the Shadow fae and the Dreamers ran even deeper than their enmity with the Court of Sky.

Cozette arched her brow, though, and Lorna got the sense she knew there was more to it. But she didn't push. She only gestured to the rows of shelves on the far side of the room and said, "It seems Lord Vargas has given you a well-stocked library. Do you enjoy reading?"

This time the smile that crossed Lorna's face was genuine. "Oh, very much so."

"As do I. Where I come from, the Glass City, we have

a building so tall, it nearly touches the stars, with row upon row, floor upon floor, filled with all manner of books and scrolls from all the courts and even the elves. Perhaps one day we can visit there together."

Lorna had long wished to see the Glass City in person, but now at the mention, her blood ran cold as the vision from her dream rushed back. Blue flames and explosions. Shattering glass and that all-devouring blinding whiteness.

She suppressed a shudder. She wasn't sure she'd ever be able to think of the Dreamer's stronghold without a flash of fear surging through her again.

But to Cozette, she only said, "I'd like that very much," and attempted to keep her smile from contorting into a grimace.

Again, Lorna got the sense that Cozette could tell she wasn't being entirely forthcoming, but she let it slide. If the Dreamer was nosing around in Lorna's head, she certainly didn't sense anything.

Cozette curtseyed. "I'll leave you in peace now. If you need anything, even just someone to talk to, I'll be right next door."

She bowed low and disappeared down the hall, leaving Lorna in the doorway, staring after her. The rune in her palm pulsed with pleasant warmth, and she knew what it was telling her—this woman could be a friend to her.

Lorna's sleep was deep and dreamless following Cozette's visit. When she awakened hours later, she wondered if the Dream fae had secretly used her strange powers to lull the torment in her mind so she could rest.

Stretching, Lorna found her wings were still sore from her long journey, and her melancholy at the loss of Osiris lingered. Still, she felt improved enough to strip off her soiled garments and clean herself up in the large porcelain tub she found in the water room adjacent to her bedchamber.

Upon emerging, she discovered a neat stack of clothing on the dresser nearest the door. When had they been brought to her? While she bathed? While she slept? She would have to remember to lock the door in the future. She valued her privacy too much to have servants wandering in and out of her rooms on a whim.

Removing one garment from the pile, Lorna shook it out to find it similar in style to her own robes, though blue rather than black with the silver-winged sigil of the Sky Court embroidered on the breast. The fabric was different, she realized as she pulled it over her head, soft and gauzy, too close to transparent for her taste.

But she supposed beggars couldn't be choosers as she stared at her reflection in the full-length looking glass. Having had nothing but a small mirror in her tiny domicile, it was strange to see her whole self staring back at her. Odder, still, to see herself dressed in these pale colors. Lorna had only ever worn black. Her sister's color and her court's.

This is who you are now, Lorna told herself, trying to make herself believe that if she tried, she could fit in here, though in her heart, she knew she would never truly be one of the Sky fae.

She would be an outsider, no matter what colors or crest she wore. But then, hadn't that always been the case? Even in the Shadow Court, Lorna had been different from the others. She could only hope here she would be less reviled for it.

But that remained to be seen.

And as Lorna stared at the woman she would have to become in her new clothes, the dream from the previous day plagued Lorna once more. She had hoped it would pass in that way dreams often do, but now, in the light of day, with sunlight streaming through the frosted glass window, she knew it was more than just the ravings of a mind delirious with stress and exhaustion.

It had been a vision.

But if she had glimpsed the future last night, what was she to do about it? Could the web of Fate be changed? The Elves thought not, based on most of her past readings. And if she couldn't alter or stop the events she'd witnessed from happening, why show them to her? What was she meant to do with knowledge?

Lorna was still staring into the mirror without seeing, brooding on what Fate and the goddess wanted of her, when a sharp rap sounded on her chamber door.

She started and turned to see Varik Skyborn, the Skylord's errant son, leaning with one elbow pressed against the door frame, his pale silver-flecked eyes raking her from head to toe.

"You clean up nicely," he declared, a smug grin pulling at the corners of his blue-tinged lips.

Clad in silver armor similar to his sister's, with his white-blonde hair pulled back in a ponytail, Varik cut a striking image, and for a beat, Lorna could only stare at him.

Then dismay overpowered her surprise, for he had no business bursting into her room without an invitation.

Forcing words out was a struggle. Lorna would have preferred to vanish in a puff of shadows. But she had a chance at forging a new life here. And in this new incarnation, she would not be the whipping the girl, the coy creature who tolerated every abuse others bestowed upon her.

Here, things would be different.

So when she said, "In the Shadow Court, one knocks before entering a lady's chambers. Perhaps the courtesies are not observed in the Court of Sky?" her voice wavered only slightly.

Varik's grin widened, flashing his brilliant white teeth. "My father always said I lack social graces," he said with a flippant boyish charm that Lorna found at once disarming and irritating because it sent a pang straight through her heart.

Though they looked nothing alike, something in Varik's teasing demeanor reminded her of Osiris and what she'd lost all over again.

First, her home—gone. Then her lover.

Lorna bit her cheek hard to distract herself from the hollowness in her heart and, perhaps more sharply than she'd meant to, snapped, "Are you here for a reason?"

To his credit, the grin slipped from Varik's face, and he actually looked chastened as he said, "My father asked me to invite you to breakfast in the great hall. After which, he would have words with you."

Lorna knew she couldn't decline, so she followed Varik down the winding halls. They were heading lower, she assumed, to the same level the throne room was on. While she knew she wasn't being led to a dungeon—for the prisoners in the Sky Court were held high in a tower —anxiety still needled her. The lower they descended, the harder it was to shake the memory of the passages leading down to the Undercity.

It looked completely different, all white and shimmering, but the sensation was the same—the descent.

And then there were the eyes. Around every corner stood a pair of guards, resplendent in silver armor, and their eyes followed her. Lorna wasn't sure whether their gazes were as mistrustful and suspicious as they seemed or if she imagined it. All she knew was her discomfort and awkwardness grew with each passing set of eyes

When they finally came to a stop in front of a large arched doorway, her breath hitched as she tried to catch it and slow it to a more natural rhythm. She didn't want to pass out upon entering the room.

Varik turned to look at Lorna, cocking his head to one side. Perhaps he noticed her trembling or the nervous way she worried her lower lip between her teeth or heard the ragged sound of her breath. Whatever it was, for once, he didn't look so smug.

Studying her with mixed curiosity and concern etched on his alarmingly handsome face, he asked, "Is everything all right?.

Lorna scoffed at him. "Does it matter? If I say, 'No, I'm not okay,' what will you do? Ignore the Skylord's order and bring me back to my chambers?"

She was surprised by the harshness in her tone, and

Varik must have been too. He blinked, rubbing the pale, downy stubble on his jaw and looking uncertain.

Then he flashed that radiant smile all the Skyborns seemed to possess and declared, "Actually, yes. That's exactly what I would do, my Lady."

Lorna rolled her eyes. "And when your father asks why you didn't do as he commanded and bring me to him? What then?"

Varik's expression shifted to his sly smirk as he lifted his shoulders in a blasé shrug and haughtily said, "I'd tell him to get buggered. Then he'd call Braedin and have him haul me off to help muck stables or something as punishment for my disrespect."

Varik paused as if gauging Lorna's reaction. He went on when she shook her head and rolled her eyes a second time. "You act as if you've never defied your father before."

He seemed to immediately recognize his mistake when Lorna's face fell—she'd told him already she did not know her father—and he quickly covered with, "Or more like you think I've never defied mine. Come now. You saw us together in his throne room. Surely you can see the way it is. He makes the rules; I break them. Not all of us simply do what we're told, Lorna Blackburn."

Varik winked and reached out, tucking a stray tendril of Lorna's long dark hair behind her ear. She was genuinely bewildered that this young man could so fearlessly and intentionally disregard the potential wrath of someone as powerful as his father.

And for his part, Varik seemed almost as baffled by her confusion over his reaction.

The two stared at each other for what felt like an age, unsure what to do next, until Lorna finally said, "Well, I'm as fine as I can be expected to be, all things considered." Her stomach rumbled, and she blushed, but a little smile cracked unbidden as she said, "Though I guess I am a little hungry."

Varik chuckled and shook his head, then bowed low to Lorna. "Now you're speaking my language, Lady Blackburn."

He rose, opened the door, and gestured, saying, "Ladies first."

Lorna hesitated. What was she about to walk into?

Sensing her unease, Varik leaned in close to her. Too close for comfort. She could smell his stormy, rain and burning ozone scent as he whispered, "Go ahead. They don't bite. Except maybe my sweet sister... but she seems to like you much more than she does me."

Lorna took a deep breath, trying to steady her shaking, and crossed the threshold. There was a clattering of silverware against porcelain as the conversation in the room abruptly ceased. Four sets of eyes stared at her— Lord Vargas, Violetta, Cozette, and the stepbrother, Braedin.

Lorna's face turned ruddy beneath their gazes. She hated attention and wanted to disintegrate into a puff of shadows or melt into the floor.

But then Varik's hand was on the small of her back, guiding her forward as he said, "And I thought I was the rude one. Don't you know better than to stare?"

He sat down across from Violetta and patted the empty seat next to him. And by the time Lorna lowered herself into it, the awkward moment had passed, and so had her trembling.

Lorna stared down at her plate. Was one person expected to eat so much? It was piled high with meat, eggs, and various other delicacies. Overwhelmed but not wanting to appear ungrateful, she speared whatever the confection of a pastry was with her fork, trying not to look confused as she brought it to her mouth and took a tentative bite.

Lorna had to force herself to swallow the moan building in her throat. Buttery and flaky, a powder of white sweetness dusted over the crust that melted in her mouth.

This was *breakfast?*

In the Shadow Court, they had gruel and black bread every single day without variation. Maybe a dollop of butter to celebrate a momentous occasion like a military victory. Ereda claimed rich food turned you soft.

She was almost in a trance, savoring the explosion of flavors on her tongue when Violetta addressed her from across the table. "You're looking better this morning, Lady Blackburn."

Lorna froze mid-swallow and forced herself to choke down her mouthful of food, then quickly dabbed at her lips with her napkin to remove any stray spun sugar, worrying over her manners. She was used to eating alone in her room, not surrounded by strangers.

Royal strangers, she reminded herself, which only made her more nervous.

"Thank you. The rest helped. And the food is delicious. I appreciate the kindness you've shown me. I hope to one day repay it," she said sincerely, if a little stiffly.

Vargas nodded while slicing a fat sausage into bite-size pieces.

"Well, you'll be happy to know I've received news that might please you from the Shadow Court." His tone was deceptively casual.

Lorna's heartbeat picked up, and her hands shook. Her fork hit the table with a clatter, but she barely even noticed the faux pas and only dimly registered that everyone was staring at her again.

"News? What sort of news?" she asked, her voice breathy and strangled.

She prayed it would be what she hoped it was. That Osiris was safe; Vargas had brokered a deal, and would join her soon.

Vargas nodded slowly. His eyes lifted from his plate to meet hers.

"Our mutual friend, the emissary, is alive."

Lorna's breathing quickened, and she had to fight her tears to keep her tears from spilling. He was alive. And if he was alive, surely she would see him again soon. The memory of his face in the cave swam behind her eyes, and her breath hitched in her throat.

Suddenly, under the table, Lorna felt something touch her foot, caressing up and down, and she nearly leapt out of her skin as she was brought back to herself. In her peripheral vision, she saw Varik staring at her with that smug look on his face again.

Across the table, Vargas furrowed his brow. "Aren't you happy to hear this news?" he inquired.

Lorna shook her head to clear it, ignoring the obnoxious boy seated next to her and returning her attention to the Skylord. "Oh yes," she breathed. "I don't think I've ever been so happy in all my life. When will he be arriving here?"

Vargas's eyes suddenly went hard as diamonds, and something menacing flashed in them as he shook his head. "He won't be. Osiris Bane will remain in the Shadow Court indefinitely."

A scream welled up inside Lorna that she knew she couldn't release. Not now. Not here, not at the breakfast table. She was not in a position to question the Skylord and ought to just be grateful he had allowed her to stay and happy that Osiris was alive at all.

Still, she couldn't help but ask, "Why?" in a whisper.

Vargas seemed as surprised as Lorna that she dared to ask. But after a long, uncomfortable pause, he explained, "He asked that he be permitted to remain in the Court of Shadows to serve your sister and that another be appointed emissary to the Sky Court."

Lorna's vision shuddered, and the room around her spun; this time, she couldn't restrain herself from shouting.

"No! You don't understand! This is some trick of Ereda's. Osiris would never, ever ask to remain in the Shadow Court. He would want to be here by my side. Osiris loves me!" Her voice was shrill, and without even realizing what she was doing, she pounded her fist on the table, making the settings rattle.

Tiny plumes of shadow peeled away from the walls,

drifting around Lorna in undulating waves she was powerless to harness.

It wasn't the Skylord who interrupted Lorna's tantrum. Instead, Violetta snapped, "Don't be a fool. Can't you see? He was playing both sides. He didn't love you. He was promised a reward to bring you to us. And now that he's lost that opportunity, he realizes the jig is up. Soon there will be war. No more playing both sides against one another. No more safe passage between the courts. Osiris Bane never loved you. Osiris Bane used you. Just as he uses everyone."

Could it be true? *No. Impossible. That night in the cave, that was real. That was true,* Lorna thought.

Aloud, she only whimpered, "He loved me," covering her tear-streaked face with her hands, unable to control the shuddering sobs that wracked her body.

"Goddess, sweet sister. Was that really necessary?"

Lorna heard Varik speak next to her and felt his hand rub her back. But it was as if everyone in the room was very far away. In another realm entirely.

The burning of the rune on Lorna's palm and a voice so soft, yet somehow able to carry above the din in the room and the screaming in her head, brought her back to herself.

Pay it no mind. They don't know everything. Vargas and Violetta spend too much time on matters of state to even know what love is. They are jaded and cold. Open your eyes. And take a deep breath.

Something was disconcerting about the voice, but Lorna couldn't figure out what it was until she hiccupped and cracked her eyelids open. Cozette was hovering beside her, hands rubbing her back in consolation. And Lorna realized she hadn't spoken aloud. The words she said had existed only in her head. The others had not heard.

Across the table, Violetta's face was set in a grimace despite not hearing Cozette's rebuke. Likely she knew of the Dream fae's talents and presumed what had happened.

Violetta's voice softened when she spoke, but there was still a chill in it. "You have my apologies, Lady Lorna. I did not mean to–"

She got no further than that. "Go to your chambers at once, Violetta, and stay there until you learn to mind your tongue. Between your inconsiderate insolence and your brother's self-absorbed impulsiveness, I don't know which of you is worse," Vargas thundered, glaring at his daughter, disgust etched on his aged face.

Violetta rose and inclined her head deferentially to her father, looking chastised as she crossed the dining room. But as she reached the arched doorway, she turned around and said, "I only spoke the truth. And everyone in here knows it. She is weak. Broken. Coddling her won't make her stronger. She needs to know how the world works."

Violetta's words sounded so much like Ereda's that Lorna's breath hitched again, and the wellspring of her tears renewed. Even here, so far from home and her sister, this warrior woman thought she was weak. It was just as her sister said. She was useless. Pathetic.

Lorna was on the verge of breaking down again, her

breaths coming in short, quick huffs when Cozette's words flooded her mind once more.

Who is she to decide what you are? Has she ever been beaten to within an inch of her life? Fled many miles across the mountains, leaving all she knows behind? Has she ever lost the man she loves? Violetta has strength in arms, but you have a strength of spirit. Do not let others' views of you shape what you believe about yourself.

How does she know all those things about me? Lorna wondered. Had Cozette simply reached into her mind to dredge out her past trauma? If you'd asked her, Lorna would have said she thought she would feel violated by someone doing something like that, and knowing so much about her.

But she didn't.

She felt consoled. Because Cozette spoke the truth.

Lorna's rune pulsed with warmth, reassuring her again that this woman was a friend. Perhaps the only one she had now. She sniffled, released a ragged sigh, and looked up, forcing a smile at the Skylord.

"I am sorry for my outburst. It was unexpected news. I find all the sudden changes lately have left me a bit emotionally unhinged."

Before Vargas could respond, Varik, seated beside Lorna, scoffed. "Violetta is a bitch–" he started, but the Skylord silenced him with a steely-eyed look.

"I will not have you speak ill of your sister. You're both thorns in my side, so neither has room to speak of the other," the Skylord snapped. Then he turned to Lorna. "What Violetta gave you was her opinion–"

"Which she ought to have kept to herself," Varik

muttered under his breath, earning him another warning glare from his father.

"—just as you ought to keep yours to yourself. Do you want to be banished to your chambers as well?"

For a moment, Varik looked like he would argue with his father, but in the end, he bit his sharp words back and only said, "No, father."

The Skylord's relief at Varik's acquiescence was palpable as the tension relaxed his facial muscles. He nodded his head, lifted his fork, and said, "Good. Let us not let this food go to waste. Eat up, then we shall go to the war room to discuss further."

As delicious as the food still looked and smelled, the knowledge that Osiris would not be joining her and the episode with Violetta had stolen Lorna's meager lose her appetite. She tried to focus on the positives - her lover was alive - but the seeds of doubt had been sewn and burned like a pit of dread, making her stomach. Feeling morose, she pushed her food around on her plate with her fork, going through the motions until the moment she'd known was coming arrived.

Vargas took the last swallow from his chalice, set it down on the table, and said, "We've tarried here long enough. We have plans to make. To the war room, Lady Blackburn, Varik."

Varik?

Lorna didn't have time to consider the Skylord's reasons for inviting his son along because Varik immediately got to his feet and took Lorna's hand in his, his grip firm, his skin cool, as he placed a kiss on her knuckles.

"Come, my lady." Varik gave her a roguish wink,

helped her to her feet, then led her out of the great hall through a door opposite the one they came in through.

Fortunately, there was no descent this time. Lorna trailed behind Varik, still hand in hand, down a single corridor with the same swirled marble floors and white walls found everywhere in the Sky Tower, but not far. They passed only a few doorways before Varik led Lorna through an open one on the right.

With the typical flourish Lorna was becoming accustomed to, though she wasn't sure whether she found it charming or irritating, Varik gestured for her to enter first.

And when she did, she let out a gasp of surprise. The war room was shaped like an octagon, with walls almost entirely of glass. She could sense the magic that made them opaque to anyone outside who might try to spy, but allowed those within to see for miles in any direction.

In the center was a table, a slab of pearly white marble cut into the shape of the Realms, with borders and topography of all the courts painted in great detail. Tiny statuettes that Lorna presumed represented armies were arrayed around it, and she was fascinated by the intricacies of their carved details.

"Have a seat," Vargas said, gesturing at a chair across from him at the table.

Varik was there quickly to pull her seat out and give her a smooth wink that brought unexpected and unwanted butterflies to her stomach.

He's just an arrogant child, Lorna told herself. *And*

*besides, my heart belongs to Osiris. I will never believe what
Violetta said was the truth.*

Varik took a seat beside her, and when Lorna came
out of her thoughts of Osiris, she found the Skylord's son
had shifted his seat unnecessarily close to hers. So close
that every draft from the large windows sent his scent
wafting to her anew.

She would have moved farther away had Vargas not
cleared his throat and spoken.

"I'm sure you've heard that the Shadow empress,
your sister, has called a Reckoning, with the presence of
all the Lords and Ladies of the courts requested?" The
Skylord's eyes were stormy as he awaited her response.

Lorna nodded uncertainly, wondering where this line
of questioning was going. If he hoped to learn Ereda's
intentions, Lorna would not be much help. They had
barely spoken of the event before everything had come
crashing down around Lorna, and she'd had to flee.

All the same, she had to say something, so she swallowed her and explained, "My sister had mentioned it to
me. I had hoped she might change her mind once I was
gone, as much of the discussion hinged on a certain scroll
and a prophecy. And with me gone, the prophecy–"

Vargas interrupted. "I am an ancient being. I have
seen hundreds of prophecies come to fruition. I can tell
you that no matter what move you make, the Fates will
do what they will. Your exodus will have no bearing on
the path of the stars. If a thing is meant to come to pass,
it will, and we are all helpless to stop it. Just as your sister
insists on the Reckoning, even now that you are here.'

Lorna shivered as the memory of her dream—exploding glass, lightning strikes, sheer terror—flashed again in her mind. She tried to convince herself it was a chill from the drafty room that suddenly walked cold fingers up her spine. But she knew it was something more, and the rune sent a sluice of ice through her veins as reinforcement.

Seeming not to notice Lorna's sudden unease, Vargas went on, "As I'm sure you know, there can only be one reason for your sister to call such an event."

Lorna's fingers worked her robes anxiously, and she gnawed her lower lip, knowing what the Skylord would say even before he said it. But when the words fell from his lips, it still felt like a thousand-pound weight was dropped onto her chest.

"War," he said, then continued, "A war in which, in some way, all the courts will play a role. And so, my children will you."

The Skylord's gaze shifted from Lorna to Varik, then back again, and Lorna's ears rang like an alarm sounding in her skull.

What would he ask of her, and what did Varik have to do with it?

"You will come to the Reckoning with me, Varik, and Violetta," Vargas announced, with a command that warned Lorna not to argue with his decree.

And she did not. She only blinked in confusion. *Why?* was what she wanted to ask, but Lorna knew better than to question Vargas's directive, particularly after her outburst earlier. The last thing she wanted was for the Skylord to decide she wasn't worth the trouble to keep around. She could wind up in chains in the Sky Tower's high dungeon or, worse, banished.

She knew there was nowhere left for her to go. She had no friends and, without Osiris, no connections. Vargas might as well simply hand her back to Ereda if he ousted her from his court.

And the Skylord knew it too.

So, instead of expressing her doubts, Lorna bowed her head and said, "I will serve you in whatever capacity I can," and bit her tongue to avoid saying more.

Vargas nodded, but his expression was still stern, and Lorna knew there would be more to it than sitting beside him as a figurehead at the meeting of the Lords and Ladies.

"Excellent. Then you'll be agreeable to my next proposition," the Skylord declared, then paused.

The silence stretched out uncomfortably, and as it did, she sensed Varik draw closer to her. His cool yet electric aroma teased her with thoughts of crackling lightning, the tangy scent of snow about to fall, and windswept fields.

Why does he sit so near? Lorna wondered.

When the Skylord spoke again, the answer was made clear.

"I would betroth you to my son, Varik. It would be better if it could be Violetta since she is my heir. But the other courts would never accept such a pairing between two girls. So it will be Varik."

Lorna's mouth fell open as she whipped her head around to stare at Varik Skyborn. He wore a sly smile on his boyishly handsome face, like a shadow cat who had gotten into the cream but knew he would suffer no punishment for it.

She nearly choked, just trying to suck in a deep, steadying breath. Betrothed? To this insolent, brash boy who was barely more than a child? How could she agree to such a thing when she still mourned so deeply for the loss of her true love, Osiris?

Sensing that she was foundering, Vargas added, "Of course, you won't be wed until your sister is overthrown. We can not commit to any one course of fate too early. But we will make a grand show of announcing that you will be soul bound to Varik soon at the Reckoning. Then you two will sit at my right-hand side, a testament to the unity of Shadow and Sky that I can offer the realms should they ally with me and not your sister."

It should have relieved Lorna to hear that the marriage was at least not imminent; Vargas might see another path forward yet. Still, she could not shake the feeling that all her free will was slipping through her fingers, her decisions stolen from her, her autonomy sacrificed to prophecies and plots.

And the threads of the web the Skylord was weaving were becoming clear to Lorna now.

Instead of a single court to rule over for all time, Vargas would risk all to build a legacy for his children by claiming two. Violetta, his daughter, would remain the heir to Sky. And Varik, his son, would wed Lorna and their children, should they have them, would inherit the Court of Shadow through her bloodline.

But surely he must know it will never work, Lorna thought.

The denizens of the Shadow Court would never welcome Lorna as their empress with open arms. Even if, by some miracle, Vargas managed to unseat Ereda, the people would never view Lorna as anything but a turncoat.

They would balk at the mere idea of a ruler who fled to the Court of Sky and took up arms against her own. They would rebel and kill her before the crown even touched her brow.

Better not to say that, though. There would be time, she decided. Time enough to make the Skylord recognize this was vanity and folly.

For now, Lorna gave Vargas a submissive bow of her head and tried to ignore the pressure of Varik's gaze on her as she said, "It is a stronger match than I could ever have imagined for myself."

The Skylord smiled, a sly, greedy thing that Lorna recognized as the very same expression her sister often wore when Lorna bent to her will. Power, she realized, had the same capacity to corrupt, no matter who chanced to wield it. This silver Lord and her black-hearted sister were not so different in their cores as they appeared at first glance.

She wondered what schemes the Shadow empress was doubtless concocting, even as they spoke to counter Vargas's moves in this grand game they played that would no doubt soon turn into a war.

Again Lorna felt the sting of loss, wishing Osiris was here. He would know more of her sister's machinations. And he would never stand for the Skylord's manipulating her into a loveless soul binding.

Perhaps it's better he's not here, Lorna thought. Had Osiris been privy to Vargas's soul-binding proposal, his response would likely have resulted in his head being removed from his shoulders.

Unless Violetta was right, and he knew all along and only pretended—

Lorna's thought was cut short by Varik, who was on his knees before her. Lorna had no idea how or when he'd dropped to them. His voice wavered as he said, "My lady, it is an honor and a gift that you have accepted my father's proposition."

And to Lorna's surprise, the Skylord's son didn't look so cocky or brazen anymore. Varik's lips were drawn in a tight line as he blinked up at her through the thick fringe of his pale lashes, and his words sounded forced and too formal.

They aren't his words, Lorna realized. Varik Skyborn had fed a script. He was probably as much a pawn in his father's elaborate scheme as she was, which could work in her favor. If Varik was as unsure and reluctant about the soul binding as she was, perhaps they could work together to prevent it. She might be able to work with that in the days ahead.

But she was staring at him, pondering, and her lack of response made the air go stale around them. So Lorna forced out, "May the Goddess Xennia bless our future union," and pressed her fingers to her lips, then touched his brow, as she knew was customary when accepting a proposal.

Varik didn't smile but remained rigid on his knees while Vargas clapped his hands, a bit mockingly by

Lorna's estimation. She imagined he enjoyed seeing his wayward, difficult son finally forced to do his bidding and wondered what threat Vargas held over Varik that had coerced him.

"Very good children. Already you play your roles well," the Skylord said.

Varik got to his feet and turned to face his father. Even with a view of only his profile, Lorna could see the insolent look she was accustomed to had returned to his handsome face.

"May I be free of my insufferable stepbrother's constant shadowing, then? I have done your will without complaint." Varik did not mask the bitterness in his voice.

Vargas studied his son, and Lorna prayed she would be spared the discomfort of witnessing yet another familial spat.

Finally, the Skylord shook his head and said, "After the Reckoning, I'll loosen your reins. Until then, you are still Braedon's charge."

Which begged the question that fell from Lorna's lips before she even had a chance to consider whether it was wise to interject. "When will the Reckoning be held, my Lord?"

"Three days' time," Vargas announced, then got to his feet before Lorna could even process the words. "So rest up, Lady Blackburn."

The Skylord returned his attention to his son and ordered, "Take her back to her chambers. I worry she is not yet fully recovered from the shock of her journey."

Lorna very nearly laughed out loud. Recovered? When had she had time to recover? A few hours of sleep, addled by terrifying visions and dreams, was all she'd had since she'd been brought here.

But Varik turned to her and gave her an almost imperceptible shake of the head. Warning her not to protest. Then he bent low, took her hand in his, and brushed his lips across her knuckles.

Drawing Lorna to her feet, he muttered under his breath, "Come, Lady Blackburn. Perhaps we can get to know each other a bit before this sham of a soul binding comes to pass."

Lorna did not want to get to know Varik Skyborn better any more than she wanted to be soul bound to him. But she again found herself caught up in a current she could not fight against as she followed Vargas's son from the throne room, leaving the Skylord poring over his map of the Realms.

Still, she did find she could breathe easier without the weight of Vargas's calculating gaze on her, so once they were well away from the doors and out of the Skylord's earshot, Lorna murmured a quiet, "Thank you," to Varik.

After which, Varik stopped in his tracks and turned to face her, snapping, "What in Xennia's name are you thanking me for?"

Lorna paled, and she wrung her hands, unsure what she had done to anger him. But the irritation drained from Varik's face as quickly as it had come. He rubbed the back of his neck, looking uncomfortable, and sighed.

"Look, I'm not the man for someone like you, Lorna," Varik said, pensive. At first, Lorna thought to be offended, but then he went on. "I'm not the man for anyone, but especially not for someone like you. My only pleasures in life are whoring and drinking and carousing with the rabble. You don't seem like the sort who'd be interested in such misadventures."

Just like that, the desperate, self-deprecating tone was gone, replaced with a sneer and Varik's usual air of arrogant indifference.

It's his armor, Lorna suddenly realized. *Just as I withdraw from others and lock myself away to hide how unworthy I fear I am, Varik dons the mask of egotism to hide the truth. Deep down, he fears the same thing as me. That he's not good enough.*

She kept those thoughts to herself but shrugged and said, "Just because that's the way you've always been doesn't mean you need to stay that person forever. You can choose to be a different man. A better man. People can change."

Varik ripped a hair through his long silver hair. For a fleeting moment, he looked vulnerable and childlike again, and Lorna willed him to open himself up to her. If she could only get past that wall... maybe there could be something there. Friendship, if not love.

But in the end, Varik's expression hardened, and he only scoffed. "The thing is, Lady Blackburn... I never said I wanted to be a better man. I don't want to change."

He tossed his long silver hair, turned away from Lorna without waiting for a reply, and began walking. Lorna hurried to keep up with his long strides, the rest of their progress silent until they reached the door to her chambers.

They walked in silence, Lorna's head spinning.

Would she really have to soul-bind herself to this beautiful but arrogant, indifferent man? Was this the cost of her safety? Was it worth it?

Varik stopped in front of her chamber door and opened it. Lorna was about to slip inside the room wordlessly. But as she moved to pass by Varik, he reached out and stopped her with a hand on her shoulder, turning her to face him.

"I think you are very beautiful, Lorna Blackburn. And strong to have endured what you have. I just wanted you to know that at least there is that."

His eyes were bright but not avaricious like his father's. Varik was hungry for something, but it wasn't power or control. Not a sexual appetite either.

Lorna stared at Varik, searching for words but finding none as she contemplated the walking contradiction that was the Skylord's son.

Love, she thought, recalling his words on the day they met. *"Two second-born children. Neither one much more than a pawn."* He feels cast aside. Just like me.

But could she ever love Varik—love anyone—as she'd loved Osiris?

No, never, she decided.

Turncloak

It was just barely midday, and Lorna was far too frazzled by the Skylord's decree about her role in the coming Reckoning to sleep when the Skylord's son left her in her room. Her nightmare tugged at her mind, and her longing for Osiris and uncertainty about Varik gnawed at her heart. She browsed the expansive library, but it soon became clear that even reading, her one true escape, would be impossible. The words and symbols danced on the pages, making no sense in her addled mind.

Meanwhile, the rune on her palm pulsed, unrelenting, driving her further to distraction. It was asking something of her. It expected her to do something, but Lorna knew not what.

She felt a strange pull to leave her chambers, very much like the force that had tugged at her when she found Muírgan Vivane's hidden scroll in Ereda's library. She knew she should not wander, but Vargas had never explicitly forbidden her from leaving her quarters, so she stepped into her doorway and peeked out into the hall.

To her left, the door that she assumed led to Cozette's chambers stood open, bathed in the same otherworldly glow as the secret compartment that had held the scroll. Destiny—guiding Lorna on a path she was helpless to step away from.

She padded to the entry and knocked lightly on the doorframe.

Cozette sat on the bed, combing her pale copper hair, and at the knock, she glanced up, giving Lorna a smile that seemed almost sad.

"Lady Blackburn, I hoped you would come. Join me," Cozette beckoned.

Lorna stepped into the chamber and crossed the room, settling herself on a wide, cream-upholstered settee at the foot of Cozette's pale lavender-dressed bed.

Cozette gave Lorna a long, probing look, then sighed. "You have many questions about what's to come, I can tell. I don't know what you've heard about the Dream fae, but some of us indeed have the power of prescience. Dark days are coming, Lady Blackburn. Not just for you, but for all of us. Many you have only just come to know are not long for this world, I fear."

Alarming words, but Lorna found she wasn't surprised. She had seen the destruction of the Glass City in her dreams. And she knew a war with the Shadow Court could come to no good end for the Sky fae. All their fates teetered on the brink of catastrophe.

Lorna's rune pulsed, acknowledging the truth of this. "I dreamed of the destruction of the Dream Court," she admitted.

Cozette nodded absently, her eyes unfocused as if she was seeing something beyond the four walls that encased them. "Not a dream. A vision. I have seen it too. But there is more than that coming, Lorna. Soon, these Realms will burn and bleed, and creatures the likes of which this world has never seen will walk its surface."

The reincarnated elf in the depths of the undercity flashed in Lorna's mind, and her stomach turned sour.

"Is there nothing we can do?" she asked.

A frown flickered on Cozette's face, then changed to the faintest hint of a smile. "The future is written in the stars, but it is not carved in stone. What we glimpse in dreams and visions is only tiny fragments of the grand scheme. Have faith that only what is meant to be will come to pass. You, me, every one of us is no more than a tiny strand in the Goddess's great plan."

How could a benevolent deity's plan permit horror the likes of which was coming? Lorna wondered, but did not ask. Instead, she wrapped her wings tightly around herself in a cocoon as if it might dull the chill of fear that had settled in her blood with Cozette's bleak words.

"I'm frightened," she confessed.

Cozette rose from the bed and came to sit beside Lorna, wrapping her in an embrace with her butterfly wings. Her touch seemed to emanate a peacefulness that swirled into Lorna's spirit, slowing her rapid heartbeat and making her eyelids heavy.

"There is much to fear. But we must also have hope.

Go now, and rest. Whatever else may be will be, but tomorrow will be a difficult day."

Back in her room after bidding Cozette farewell, Lorna drowsed. It might have been the most peaceful, undisturbed sleep of Lorna's life, but it ended far too soon. Would that she could have remained in that dreamless space, devoid of thoughts and pains for a century, but it was not to be. Her consciousness was pulled back to reality by rapping on her door.

Pale beams of sunlight leaked through the gauzy shroud of the curtains to pool on the white marble floor. Morning already? Had she slept so long? Lorna felt as if she had only just closed her eyes.

And the rays of light did nothing to brighten her dark mood. For Lorna knew what lay in the future on this day. The Reckoning.

She stretched, releasing a world-weary sigh, then struggled to find her voice, caught in a throat clenched tight with anxiety, to call, "Come in."

The door opened to reveal Violetta, her pale hair pulled back from her face in severe, elaborate braids, her eyes darkened by heavy shadows as if she hadn't slept a wink the night before.

Lorna watched the Skylord's daughter warily as she took a tentative step into the room, then said, "I wanted to apologize. I had no right to say the things I did at breakfast yesterday. It is a difficult time to be the heir to the Sky Court, and some days, I fear I'm watching it all slip away, losing the charmed life of my girlhood."

Violetta furrowed her brow and shook her head. "But that's no excuse. I blame your sister for what I fear will soon befall us. And I took it out on you. It was wrong of me."

The heir to the Court of Sky stood rigid and formidable in her armor. To Lorna, she looked more like a statue carved of ice than a woman. But she recognized the burden on Violetta's shoulders and accepted that there was no crime in speaking what one believed was the truth.

So Lorna nodded at Violetta and gave her a strained, fragile look of compassion. "Believe me when I say, though we are blood, I love my sister no more than you do. Let's not quarrel amongst ourselves. We have enough enemies to contend with," she said.

That bright, glorious smile that so rarely broke the frigid surface of Violetta's face shone through, making Lorna wonder what the Skylord's daughter would have grown to become had she not always had the weight of Vargas's expectations pressing down on her.

Then it faded, slipping away like a half-remembered dream. Violetta was once more the stern and unyielding warrior Lorna had met outside the Sky Tower walls. "I agree," she said stiffly, then went on. "We have far to travel and likely nothing good to meet us when we arrive. Wear the new blue and silver gown in the wardrobe. My brother will be back to escort you to the caravan in an hour's time."

Violetta did not wait for Lorna to respond but turned and left, closing the door behind her, leaving Lorna to an oppressive silence that made her mind and her heart race like a hummingbird's.

Lorna reluctantly peeled herself out of bed, crossed

the room, and opened the wardrobe. Hanging there was a new gown she'd never seen before - nor had she seen one like it.

Unlike the long, loose-fitting robes she had worn since arriving in Sky and at the Shadow Court, the gown fit tightly with long, bell sleeves and made of a thick, iridescent blue fabric. White leather pauldrons with a silver fringe were mounted on the shoulders, and a row of buttons fastened it up the front, all the way to the high neckline that covered the throat.

Not a gown for a ball or a social gathering. These were the trappings of war. Armor, for a woman who fought with magic rather than a sword.

"Are you ready, my lady?" Varik's voice filtered through the closed door.

Lorna took a ragged deep breath and glanced at herself once more in the mirror. She barely recognized herself in the gown with her hair plaited similarly to Violetta's, high and tight. Where was the bookish girl all in black, with her hair long and loose, who spent her days hiding away with her nose in a book?

Surely this woman who gazed back at her was some other creature entirely.

In the pauldroned gown with the chainmail bodice, Lorna looked... imposing.

If only she felt that way, but she was still terrified. More frightened now than she'd ever been to see her sister. Her whole body trembled as she made her way to her door with halting steps and opened it.

Varik stood there, looking like a white knight in his voluminous ivory cloak draped over silver armor that appeared freshly forged. A helm adorned with white wings covered his silver hair with the visor pulled back to reveal a smile.

But Lorna could tell from how it didn't make it to his eyes that it was false. Varik Skyborn was scared, too, whether he admitted it or not.

"We need to go now," he said softly, and Lorna only nodded, not trusting herself to speak without her voice breaking.

Their walk to the courtyard passed in silence, lost in a miasma of worrying thoughts. Lorna's sister would be at the Reckoning, seated at the same table as her. Lorna would have to see her face-to-face again after all that had happened—something she had hoped never to do. She hoped Ereda would not openly attack her before all the Lords and Ladies... But Lorna knew her sister well enough to recognize the lengths she would go to for revenge when she believed she was wrong.

And to Ereda, Lorna was the worst kind of traitor.

The Skylord would also announce her impending soul binding to Varik in front of the Lords and Ladies of all the Courts. It would infuriate the Shadow Empress, but more than that, Bleakhart had been right about one thing—everyone save the Dreamers reviled the mixing of blood between the courts. How would she survive the looks of revulsion, the judgment in their eyes?

And worst, what dark days would the Ereda's Reckoning usher in? What horror and brutality would she unleash on the Realms when the other Courts refused to bend to her will?

"Go ahead, Lady Blackburn."

Lorna hadn't even realized they'd reached the exit until Varik spoke. And every muscle in her body resisted her effort to move forward and cross that threshold.

But the rune went warm with a wave of comfort that warned her, *You must. This is your destiny. You are needed here to see this thing through.*

Lorna stepped outside.

Three silver carriages flying blue flags embroidered with the white-winged sigil of Sky parked in the court-yard, pulled by pegasi, white as the driven snow, their manes and tails braided with bells and strung with silver ribbons. Pixies sat on the soft white front cushions, shimmering in myriad colors, holding the winged horses' reins.

The sight took Lorna's breath away, and for a moment, all her fears were forgotten, faced with the beauty of the Sky Court's royal caravan.

Then the Skylord turned around where he stood, fussing over a bridle, his drawn face and furrowed brow reminding Lorn that this was no joy ride. They might very well all of them be flying straight into their doom.

"Good of you two to join us," Vargas barked with a scowl.

He looked Lorna up and down, assessing her in the new, martial-looking gown, and clucked his tongue approvingly.

"Don't slouch," Lord Vargas ordered, and Lorna flushed with embarrassment, straightening at once. "You two"— the Skylord shifted his gaze to his son and jerked his chin toward the second carriage—"will ride together. Violetta and I will be in the lead. Servants in the back.

And I don't care how you feel about one another. When we reach the Circle, you'll act like you're madly in love."

To his credit, Varik didn't smirk at the notion, though Lorna got the feeling he wanted to.

Vargas had turned away and was about to step inside the lead carriage when something occurred to Lorna. Without thinking, she blurted, "Will Cozette be coming?" hoping the answer was yet. Not only was the Dream fae a friend, but her mind-reading powers and her soothing presence would be helpful for all parties present in her mind.

But Vargas snorted and shook his head. "I can't very well parade my paramour around in the company of Lords and Ladies. Cozette will remain here, as befits her station."

That is a mistake, Lorna thought at once, and the rune went fire hot in agreement. She opened her mouth to say so, but Vargas didn't give her a chance.

"Do you have something more to say on the matter?" The Skylord's eyes were hard, making it clear he wasn't interested in further discussion.

So, Lorna murmured, "No, my Lord."

"Excellent. Then let's get on with this."

Without another word spoken, they all boarded the carriages.

The Beginning of the End

The ride passed in tense silence. Varik, ordinarily so brash and talkative, was somber and withdrawn, sharpening his dagger on his whetstone.

Lorna tried to watch the scenery fly by—the tall sentinel pines and the wide meandering river, blue, not red like the waters that ran from Funeral Mountains into the Shadow Court—but the scraping of the metal against the stone was enough to drive her half mad.

Finally, to put an end to the torment, she asked Varik, "Have you ever seen the Circle before?"

Lorna herself had not. The Circle, like the Glass City, was another place Lorna had read about but never beheld herself. Once, it was the sacred space of the Elves, located on the border of the Sky and Fire Courts. But many years ago, early in the Fae conquest, the Fire fae had driven the elves out of the region.

And so, it became the sacred space of the fae. Though, if the writings were true, the elves took some of the magic with them when they fled. It was said that the Circle functioned as a portal within the Ethereal Realms and beyond while still in elven hands.

Now, it was only a ruin, a series of massive moonstones arranged in a ring, the magic all gone.

"Of course I have. A hundred times on patrol."

To 'Lorna's relief, he at least stopped fussing v with the dagger and the stone as he bragged.

Varik leaned back in his seat, kicking his legs out like a stretching cat, his chainmail boot brushing 'Lorna's calf. She flinched back from the contact.

Varik smirked. "You know, if 'we're going to pretend to be in love, 'you'll have to stop shying away every time I touch you."

Heat rose in 'Lorna's cheeks as she muttered, "It would seem so."

Apparently more amused by the conversation than his blade for the moment, Varik sheathed it and put away the whetstone. Then he pushed off the carriage bench and dropped down next to Lorna on the other side of the carriage.

"Let's practice," Varik said with a wicked grin that made a whole kaleidoscope of butterflies take wing in her belly.

Osiris was handsome; Lorna had recognized that since they were children. And perhaps her sorrow over the loss of her lover had blinded her to the truth about the Skylord's son before.

But now, sitting here beside him, the smell of ozone burning in the air, she recognized that Varik Skyborn was a different animal entirely. He was dangerously beautiful and disconcertingly charismatic. The kind of man who could steal your heart—then tear it out and leave you a shell with an empty space where the organ should be, bleeding out slowly and surely.

Yet you'd still come back for more.

With Varik so close, she could make out the pale blue spiderwebs of veins at his temples, so fair was his skin, and his big, expressive blue eyes seemed to shift hue from silvery to cerulean and everything in between with the changing light and his mood. She could drown in those eyes if she let herself.

A pang of guilt stabbed Lorna as Varik raised her hand, his touch cool as he traced from her brow to her cheekbone with the lightest graze of her fingers.

I do not want him. I love Osiris, she reminded herself/

Besides, falling for Varik Skyborn would be like wrapping a noose around her own neck. But if she had to pretend she did, how could she guard her heart?

"Varik, I'll put on the show. But please, don't–"

He didn't move away, instead leaning in closer. A breeze picked up in the carriage, his magic swirling through the confines, brushing Lorna's skin with tendrils as gentle as his fingers. She felt her own shadows rising, the temptation pulling them close like a shroud around her.

"This may be the end of days, Lorna Blackburn. At

least for you and me. Don't you want to feel something before you disappear into that long eternity of nothingness in the Void?"

She expected him to be wearing his seductive, insolent smirk. But he wasn't. Varik looked somber and almost pleading.

And, Goddess, in that moment, she *did* want to feel —and something passionate and unhinged stirred inside her. A longing she did not know she was capable of.

But before she could act on it, the carriage jerked to a halt, and the moment was lost as she twisted her head to look out the window and saw the standing stones.

Swathed in a low-lying fog, the Circle's stones towered fourteen feet high and spanned the length of a tourney field; the moonstones reflected the afternoon light, casting a multitude of rainbows in the hazy air around them.

A little sound of awe escaped Lorna's lips. She was so enraptured she barely noticed Varik's hand resting on her thigh.

"A beautiful backdrop for a day that promises to be full of horrors, isn't it?"

And with his words, the spell was broken, for Lorna's eye caught on the Shadow Empress's caravan. The black carriages accented with bits of bone, and the stomping, snorting night mares that drew them looked wildly out of place against the serene backdrop. Beyond, she saw the other transports—the sleighs bedecked in cockle shells and curtained with seaweed of the Sea Court, the strange, eyeless mole creatures who drew the Earth fae's unornamented wagons, fiery phoenixes tethered to great red and gold chariots from Flame, the shimmering opalescent coaches from the Court of Dreams.

They were the last to arrive.

Lorna wondered if Vargas had done that on purpose, intending a grand, dramatic entrance. To her, it seemed unwise. Alliances could be forged, and hostilities put aside with whispers during the quiet moments before the Reckoning began in earnest.

But there was naught to be done for it now.

Beside her, Varik rose, extending a hand to her. He leaned in close, his lips touching her neck as he said, "Time to play the game. May the odds be in our favor."

Lorna knew they weren't. When dealing with her sister, the odds were always stacked against you.

Her body was so tight with tension that her neck ached, and her knees threatened to buckle as they approached the Skylord's carriage.

Violetta emerged first, looking more severe and militant than ever. She did not wear a gown like Lorna's but full plate armor like her brother; her helm carried by her side. When she nodded to Lorna, she saw flames of fear in Violetta's eyes too.

"All three of you look like frightened rabbits," the Skylord growled. "You"—he jerked his chin at his daughter—"stop standing there like someone rammed a dagger up your ass. You've been practicing for this your whole life. Smile. Look gracious. Proud."

Violetta forced a smile at her father's command, but it manifested more like a grimace, nothing like the shining, radiant expression Lorna had seen grace her face before.

"And you two, get closer. At least look like you like each other," Vargas snapped.

Varik pulled Lorna gently to his side, so their hips pressed against each other. Surprisingly, she found the contact soothed her. Perhaps it served as a reminder that she wasn't alone. That whatever may come, someone stood beside her—even if he was forced to be here.

"Better. Let's get on with this, then," Vargas announced. All the bluster was gone from his voice, and he sounded weary–almost defeated.

But when he set off towards the Circle with long strides, his head was high, his back straight, and his silver circlet shone in the light.

Violetta fell into step behind the Skylord, hand resting on her sword's pommel.

And then it was Lorna and Varik's turn. He clutched her hand so tightly that she felt the bones might break, but Lorna didn't mind.

Her rune vibrated with warmth, and she knew this was right. This was where Fate needed her to be. No matter how much she dreaded what was to come.

"Just stay with me. Everything will be all right," Varik reassured her, and then he smiled.

Not forced, like Violetta's, and not his characteristic smirk. A dazzling, radiant smile that looked as natural as if he were stepping into a garden party.

And this, Lorna realized, was what made Varik Skyborn dangerous. It was why she needed to steal her heart against him.

The ease with which he lied.

The air shimmered with the thin veil of magic

remaining in the Circle. An opaque veil obscured what lay on the other side; try as she might, Lorna could not see past it. She was walking into this blind, and Lorna ground to a halt at the gap between stones they were to pass through.

She couldn't do this. Whatever the Goddess, the stars, the Fates expected of her, it was too much.

At Lorna's hesitation, Varik turned to her. His eyes were wild, like he'd burned off all his fear and was feeding on pure adrenaline now. Lorna wished she could do the same, but her heart hammered, and her palms sweat as she stood frozen, unable to make her leaden limbs obey.

Varik's gaze steadied when it connected with hers. He squeezed Lorna's hand and said, "I promise. I won't let your sister hurt you again."

Lorna swallowed hard and nodded. But she knew it wasn't that. Not really. Lorna Ereda would never lash out at her in front of all the fae nobility. Emotion was weakness to the Shadow empress.

No, something deeper held Lorna back. The knowledge that whatever happened here today would change the whole world. Not just her world, but the entirety of the Ethereal Realms. Nothing would ever be the same after this day.

Lorna felt it in her core.

"We have to go through. They're all waiting," Varik said softly, then released her hand. Wrapping his arm around her waist, he pulled her closer, then urged her on with a slight pressure at the small of her back.

Despite the screaming in her heart and mind, Lorna nodded to Varik, and they crossed the threshold. Her skin tingled faintly as the magical barrier parted for them, and the world went white for a moment, reminding her of the blankness following the explosion in her nightmare.

When her vision cleared, Lorna found herself staring directly at her sister.

The Shadow empress's cold, dark eyes burned into Lorna. She didn't wear her usual robes but tight black leather armor with bone embellishments that hugged her rail-thin frame. On another woman, it might have created the illusion of frailty. But on Ereda, with her snakes hissing in her hair, forked tongues tasting the air for the scent of fear, it made her appear even more threatening. Like a skeletal wraith.

The Empress turned her head, pretending to ignore Lorna, who followed her gaze... to see Osiris Bane standing by Ereda's side.

Their gazes locked, and Osiris's eyes flashed with something—remorse? Sorrow? It was gone so fast, Lorna couldn't say, and besides, it took all her presence of mind to concentrate on not keeling over the pain and shock cut so deep.

Why was Osiris not here with her sister, not locked away in some dungeon? Had Violetta been right all along? The world flickered, and Lorna felt a thump like a kick in the ribs, sucking all the air out of her lungs. Even through the spots dancing in her vision, Lorna could see that Osiris looked unchanged, except his emissary livery was replaced by armor bearing an emblem Lorna recognized.

The Wild Hunt insignia... My sister made him Hunt Master? After he turned me over to the Skylord.

Varik pinched her hard just beneath the ribs. "Just walk with me," he ground out through his clenched-teeth smile, his grip on her waist tightening, pressing her to move.

And somehow, Lorna did. Leaning against Varik, his presence the only thing keeping her upright, she crossed the field. They took their spot beside the Skylord and Violetta. There were no chairs, so all the Lords, Ladies, and their escorts remained standing at the points in the Circle corresponding with their Courts' geographic positions.

Was the Skylord disappointed in her performance? Lorna didn't know. She couldn't even turn her head to acknowledge the Skylord, fearing her gaze might catch again on her erstwhile lover and she would fall to pieces.

Varik's hand remained firm and steadied her at the waist as whispers and murmurs laced the air. Lorna couldn't make out a word of them. She could only hear a white noise buzz, like the hum that laces the air before an explosion.

The whispers ceased as Ereda prowled into the center of the Circle, stalking like a vulpine, teeth bared in a predatory sneer as she did a full turn. All eyes were on the empress, and her unwavering gaze met each set, holding the contact for a long moment before moving to the next.

Except for Lorna. The Shadow empress and her sister did not connect gazes, for Lorna stubbornly stared at the bright green wildflower-strewn, just trying to breathe.

The leaden weight of Varik's armored embrace seemed like the only thing tethering her to this stretch of earth.

Finally, when the tense silence seemed more than anyone could bear, Ereda spoke. "It has been many hundreds of moons since the last Reckoning was called."

Thousands, Lorna corrected in her head, but the others seemed not to care about the historical inaccuracy, and her sister was already moving on.

"So, you must be wondering what could be so imperative that I should call such a meeting face to face, between all of the fae nobility now."

Her pause for dramatic effect was interrupted by Somnium, the Lord of Dreams, standing directly across from the Sky Court delegation, who said, "I think we all know what we are doing here, Lady Blackburn. You can spare us your grand soliloquy."

Somnium's voice was placid, almost bored, as if he hadn't a care in the world. The lilt of his voice, so similar to Cozette's, caught Lorna's ear, and she looked up to get a better look at him. Young, compared to the other Lords and Ladies, with hair the color of burnished copper and bright orange and gold wings of likeness to a monarch butterfly. The only ruler who had not deigned to wear armor, instead the simple white robes of a scholar with no crown upon his brow.

Lorna and Somnium had never met, but she recognized him at once. She had seen him in her dream, standing in the Glass City.

Ereda's snakes snapped their fangs at the interruption, but her poise did not slip. Giving Somnium a nod of acknowledgment, she said, "Yes, you're right, Lord Somnium. Time is of the essence."

As she spoke, she raised a hand. Shadows coalesced in her palm. When they had pooled there, swirling black and menacing, she snapped her fingers, and they dispersed, revealing a familiar rolled scroll in the palm of her hand.

Lorna had seen the spell before. It was more a parlor trick than anything else, displacing matter in the shadows, then calling it back to form. Evidently, the fae of the other courts had not, though, for a chorus of gasps and whispers rippled through the Circle at the sleight of hand.

Only Lorna and Somnium did not respond with alarm.

Taking his cue from Somnium, once Lord Vargas shook off his surprise, he blustered. "No more smoke and mirrors, Lady Blackburn. Tell us what you want."

Ereda gave the Skylord a mocking little bow. "As you wish. This scroll,"—she unrolled the parchment, brandishing the very same document signed by Muírgan Vivane Lorna had discovered in the library—"bears a prophecy. The Dread of the Elves. It reveals the end of days for their people... but ushers in a new, golden era of prosperity for us. The fae."

The Shadow empress swept her hands in a wide circle, encompassing all the Lords and Ladies standing in the shadows of the stones. But she did not give them time to react or interrupt before going on. "This prophecy claims that a Legion Queen will be born among the fae, who will unite them under one banner.

And the lesser races, the elves and even the mortals will be vanquished once and for all. Annihilated or enslaved. No longer will their tainted blood mix with ours."

A murmur went up now. Approval from the Fire and Earth Courts, as expected. Outright disgust from Dreams and Sky.

But Lorna peeked to her left and studied Nimione, the Lady of the Undersea, with her long turquoise hair and scaled legs. She frowned uncertainly, her head cocked to the side as if she wasn't quite sure how she felt about this business.

If Vargas can win over Nimione to our side, we at least stand a chan—

Ereda interrupted her thoughts, raising the prophetic scroll high above her head and declaring, "Lords and Ladies, it is me! I am the Legion Queen the Realms have been waiting for!"

The blood drained from Lorna's face at the proclamation, and she violently shook her head, crying without thinking, "It isn't true!"

As every gaze in the room was pulled from her sister to fall on her, Lorna's skin crawled, and she longed to vanish into shadowy ether. Why had she done that? How could she have been so foolish as to draw attention to herself? She had no right to be here, was only a pawn in Vargas's game. Arm candy for his son. A silent actress in the performance.

But now she had spoken, and the Shadow empress's wrath fell upon her. Ereda barked out a laugh and turned to face Lorna, shadows darkening her gray skin until it turned to onyx. "The traitor speaks! Did you have something to say, my sweet, treacherous sister?"

"Say nothing," Varik hissed in Lorna's ear, trying to angle his body to put hers behind him.

But the same blaze that had ignited in her blood when Lorna stood up to her sister in the throne room kindled in her blood again now. She would not be swept aside and ignored this time just because the truth she spoke was inconvenient or unwanted. Not when so much hung in the balance.

Her rune throbbed as the memories of all her sister's evil schemes—the blood magic, Bleakhart's experiments, the undead fiends... but more than that, the centuries of cruelty and isolation she'd been subjected to—all rushed through Lorna's mind. And the elven rune Cruciamena —the pain bringer—burned, recognizing the pain, and turning it into strength.

Lorna straightened and lifted her chin, stepping out of Varik's embrace. "You speak lies, sister. Or you have been misinformed. Who translated the words of the prophecy for you? Bleakhart? You don't think he'll tell you anything you want to hear just to curry your favor, as I once did?"

"Lorna Blackburn, stay your tongue," Lord Vargas snarled. He took her arm and squeezed it, his face growing redder by the second.

Lorna ignored the Skylord and went on. "I have read that scroll myself, sister. Those are not the words written on it. *It* is *my* destiny to find the Legion Queen. And you are not her."

An animalistic growl came from deep in Ereda's

throat, and the sibilant hiss of her snakes mingled with it, hovering in the rapt, hushed air, eerie and hollow.

She stepped toward Lorna, scoffing. "You? Your *destiny?* And who are you? A mistake of the goddess who killed our mother. A traitorous whore who fucks errand boys and sells yourself to the highest bidder."

The words were like a swift kick to Lorna's gut. Because deep inside, that was exactly what she feared she was. She would have caved then and given in to her sister as she always did, had Varik not released her and stepped forward, so close Ereda's snakes might have bitten him had a sudden burst of wind not blown them back.

"Move away from my bride-to-be." His eyes were narrowed, and his hand rested on the pommel.

Ereda's cackle was bitter and sharp. The Lords and Ladies gasped and chattered amongst one other.

But Lorna wasn't looking at her sister anymore or at the others. For Osiris had stepped forward, and his eyes found Lorna's, anguished, even a little frightened.

He still cares for me, Lorna realized.

Whatever role he played for Ereda was not by choice, or at least not entirely. Violetta was wrong.

Osiris leaned close to Ereda and whispered something in her ear. The empress gave him an almost imperceptible nod, then waved him off. Her expression shifted back to calm imperiousness.

"Enough of this foolishness," Ereda declared with a wave of her hand. "I came here to garner your support for my Edict of Culling. The elves are a threat to our very existence. The Ethereal Realms will never be safe until all the elves, to a one, have been destroyed or enslaved. And that is what I intend to do. My armies will march, hunting them from the peaks of the Funeral Mountains to the depths of the phantasmal sea. From the heart of the forest to the lava flats. No more games, no more banter. We vote now. Are you with me or against me?"

Blood Burn

Ereda waited in the center of the Circle. Overhead, black clouds gathered, ushered in by the dark words, their shadow looming over the gathered fae, threatening a storm the likes of which had never been seen before.

Asheron Drogon, the Flamelord, stepped forward first, his hair eyes like molten gold, brassy hair streaming over his shoulders. He was a massive man with a barrel chest and a bold countenance—never one to shy away from a fight.

Lorna knew what he would say before the words fell from his tongue.

"The Elves have long been a thorn in my side. On this very spot, they slaughtered hundreds of my brethren. I will support this edict with the full might of the Flame

Court. My arms and armor are at your disposal, Empress Blackburn."

Lorna bristled but said nothing, though she knew his words were no less a lie than her sister's. Any massacre here had been justifiable. These lands had once all belonged to the elves. When the fae invaded, it was a mad dash to scrape out holdfasts. Here, Asheron had staked his claim. There had been battles and death, but the elves weren't marauding killers—they were defending themselves and what was theirs. Their homeland.

But that would be a moot point if pressed to Ereda, whose lips twitched into a tight, closed-lipped smile. She beckoned Asheron to stand beside her and said, "Excellent. Who else stands with us? Together we can bring glory, safety, and prosperity to the realms!"

The hesitation was mere moments before the twin rulers of the Earth Court stepped forward, their moves perfectly synchronized. Their insectile wings buzzed the air, their countenances gruff and all business as Aldine and Alaric both gave sharp nods of their heads.

Men of few words, the Lords of Earth said, "Aye," in unison, and nothing more.

Lorna's guts curdled inside her. Couldn't they see? The Skylord and the Dreamlord would never agree to this. This edict would cause a rift between the courts that might never be healed.

War. This can only end in war, Lorna thought. Then her gaze cut to Nimione, the Sea Queen.

She looked pensive, gnawing her lower lip as her daughters whispered back and forth. *She does not want to do this either,* Lorna realized, a tiny sprout of hope blooming inside her only to be dashed.

Ereda's had mind calculated just as Lorna's did. For once, the two sisters were not so dissimilar. She turned to Nimione and said, "And what of the Sea Court?"

Nimione stared down at her webbed feet, her color rising. Then she sighed and, in her sweet siren-song voice, answered, "The Court of Sea is isolated beneath the waves. We have no grievance with any on land, but have battles of our own to fight with the Naga and the other native species underwater. We request neutrality until such a time as we can spare men and arms to wage war on another front."

She is wise, Lorna thought. *She will not outright oppose the Shadow empress, but will not stand with those who stand against her, either.*

Then her heart chimed in, *Playing both sides, like your lover.*

For a moment, Ereda looked angry, and Lorna thought she would not honor the request for neutrality. Then Osiris, beautiful, dark Osiris, stepped up to Ereda and whispered in her ear. Lorna's breath caught in her throat as he wrapped an arm around the empress's waist. Ereda allowed no one to touch her like that.

Perhaps Violetta was not so wrong as I thought, after all.

For Osiris had always been about the climb. He would never choose the losing side. And as of now, that was where Lorna stood.

"Fair," Ereda finally declared with a curt nod. "Your request is granted."

Somnium did not wait for Ereda to call him forward. Looking as unruffled as ever, he stepped into the Circle and locked eyes with the Shadow Empress. They only glared at one another for a painful moment that seemed to stretch on for far too long.

Then, when the tension had mounted to a fever pitch, the Dreamlord finally said, "My Court has lived in harmony with the elvish folk for long centuries. We have given them a safe harbor and learned much from them over the years. The elves will not fight alone."

Her words hung in the air, and the implied threat was clear. The Dreamers had gleaned at least some secrets of magic from the elves over the years, and they would use that knowledge to aid the downtrodden people. Even if it meant standing against a coalition far greater in number.

"So, you oppose me?" Ereda's calm was unruffled; she seemed mildly annoyed if anything. Surely, she had hoped for a unified front, but she had expected this along and would not let it sway her.

"We do," Somnius affirmed.

And before the words had even left the Dreamlord's mouth, Vargas Skyborn came forward and said, "The Court of Sky stands with the Dreamers. We would not purge an entire race from the Realms simply because they are not like us. The elves have suffered enough. Let them migrate to the Courts of Dream and Sky, so we might live in peace."

It was a pretty dream, but one that could never see the light of day. At least not while Ereda was in power.

Ereda stripped one of her long, black satin gloves

from her hand and tossed it carelessly on the ground. It lay there, a black stain amid the green grass strewn with yellow dandelions and poppies as red as blood.

No one made a sound. Even the birds in the surrounding forest seemed to choke on their songs and go silent. There could be no doubt as to what the thrown gauntlet meant. Ereda need not have spelled it out, but she did anyway.

"It is war, then," the Shadow empress declared, her tone making it clear they had passed the point of negotiation.

It was done.

There would be war.

The words rang in Lorna's head long after the sound had been carried away on the wind. She'd known in her heart it would come to this, but with every fiber of her being, she had hoped there might be another way. She wanted to fall at Ereda's feet and beg her sister to reconsider. Tell her that the elves were not truly her enemies, no more than the other fae courts were.

But Lorna recognized the look in her sister's eyes. She'd seen it a thousand times before—when she learned some new spell in a scroll. When she banished her to the dungeon with Bleakhart. When she learned of the scroll and the prophecy.

Ereda's eyes shone with greed. Lust for power. The Shadow empress would not be swayed.

Across the Circle, Somnium held out his hand; Lorna assumed to remove his own glove. But no. Somnium wore no gloves. He simply extended it and waited. A high-pitched coo rolled through the air as a white blur soared through the barrier between the standing stones, and a white dove came to land on his bare hand.

The Dreamlord cupped it gently, then set it on the ground with an almost playful smile that seemed wildly out of place, given the tension was so thick one could slice it with a knife.

Lorna gaped as the bird transformed, and a gasp rippled among the Lords and Ladies, revealing a beautiful Elven woman with coils of pale hair cascading down to her hips. A circlet rested on her forehead, and she was dressed all in white—the same white robes the elves and Dreamers in Lorna's vision had worn. Her eyes, a green that could only be described as the hue of spring leaves and new grass, flitted from face to face around the Circle.

She smiled when her gaze fell on Lorna, but her expression transformed into righteous fury when she looked at the Shadow empress.

Ereda smirked, giving the elven woman an icy look, a muscle in her jaw ticking.

When she spoke, her tone was even colder than the glare. "Amabella Gracelilly. I'd hoped you'd be in chains the next time I saw you. But here you are. An uninvited guest."

"Lady Blackburn," Amabella addressed her with a nod.

"It's Empress Blackburn," Ereda corrected.

"For now." In a single smooth move, Amabella stripped her white elbow-length glove off and flung it atop the Shadow empress's.

Amabella spoke in a voice that seemed to come from all directions at once, carrying from each of the stones surrounding the Circle. "The elves and the Dreamers stand united. We will fight to prevent this reign of Shadow until every last one of us has been wiped from the face of the Realms."

Lorna trembled and clung to Varik as the stones illuminated, burning red hot around them.

And then, with a clatter, the Skylord removed his gauntlet, added it to the pile, and said, "And the Court of Sky stands with them."

Almost as one, Asheron, Aldine, and Alaric ripped off their gauntlets and tossed them at Ereda's feet. At the same time, Nimione stepped back until she almost brushed the shimmering magical boundary between the stones.

Lorna swallowed the whimper building in her throat and stared in horror at her sister, willing Ereda to say or do something to undo this disaster she had set into action.

But the Shadow empress did nothing, and the moments ticked by until she looked up from the pile of metal and cloth. For the first time, Lorna saw the glimmer of fear in her sister's eyes when she said, "It is done, then."

Then the fear passed, replaced by something Lorna was more familiar with seeing in her sister. Determination. Unyielding steadfastness.

"You will be sorry, those of you who chose the losing side. I will destroy you. This will be the end of your courts. Your blood will burn in your veins, and the shadows will swallow you whole. There will be nothing left of you by the time I am done. For you defy the Fates and stand in the way of destiny."

Suddenly the air in the Circle darkened, the shadows elongating and drawing inward away from the stones. Until they swallowed up Ereda, and the Shadow empress disappeared.

And with that, the war that would shake the Ethereal Realms to the very foundation began.

About the Author

Kate's writings interweave fantasy, dystopia, and mythology into unique, romantic tapestries. An introvert, dog mom, and freelance editor, when she's not searching for fairy circles in hopes of being transported to an enchanted kingdom, Kate is immersed in the chaos of her writing process.

She lives with her husband and her rescue dog Gracie on the banks of the Hudson in Westchester County, NY, where, alas, she has found few portals to magical realms.

Links:
Facebook group: www.facebook.com/groups/
Courtofdreams
Facebook page: www.facebook.com/katesegerauthor
Instagram: www.instagram.com/katesegerauthor
Tiktok: https://www.tiktok.com/t/ZTd3txyDD/

Also by Kate Seger

Vellas

Tales of the Fae

Poppy - A Moonlight Hospital Drama

A Demon's Scorn

Pay the Toll

Clandestine

These are My Grave Blooms

Novels

Tales of the Gloaming

Tria Ellinka

Tales of the Fae Series

The Shadow's Sister - Preorder for March 2023

Lord of Storms - Coming July 2023

The Ethereal Realms Series

The Wood Witch's Daughter

The Last Dreamer

Printed in Great Britain
by Amazon